BEGINNER BITCHCRAFT

BEGINNER BITCHCRAFT

For Diamonds in the Rough

JEWEL ALBRIGHT COHEN

Jewel Albright Cohen Publishing LLC

ISBN-13: 9780998895307
ISBN-10: 099889530X
Library of Congress Control Number: 2017906570
Jewel Albright Cohen Publishing, Waterford, MI

CONTENTS

PREFACE

My working title for this book has been *Bitch in the Burbs*. The term *working* is ironic, because the hero seems to have trouble keeping a job. Yes, each of us can be the hero of our own story. And if I'm not exactly the hero, at least no one else is holding the pen in the story of my life...anymore.

My name is Jewel, and my hidden talent is bitchcraft—the art of pissing people off using the truth. Let this be a lesson to you: never wrong a writer.

Our setting is the US Midwest. I am the bitch in the burbs. The one thing I am *not* is the victim. My greatest blessing, my tribe, lives mostly in and around metropolitan Detroit, and a few old friends and kin reside down some back-country roads in a tiny town just outside Climax called Walnut Grove. This is a story about the people who make life worth living: friends, family, neighbors, frenemies, and enemies. Picture a *Bridget Jones's Diary* made in Oakland County and blended into a survival guide. Slowly, painfully slowly, as I continue to make an ass of myself, vital lessons are learned.

In my life, I went from *being* the help to *hiring* the help—and then back to *being* the help. The days and events in which I appeared most polished represented a mind-numbing, lifeless existence. Staged, silent photos represent stifled screams. If I have learned nothing else in life, I've learned that when people are trying to suppress your voice, you have something formidable to say.

These stories speak of resilient women, a fierce sisterhood, and reaching maturity (or as close to it as we can get). Language is an effective, vital tool for dealing with emotions. However, uncomfortable words and feelings are usually kept under wraps. That will not happen here.

Lesson one—out of twenty-four in the art of bitchcraft—is to journal privately. If we said exactly what we thought and did whatever we wanted, ruinous things would assuredly happen. If we were not in actual solitary confinement, we would still scare off enough people to be forced to live a solitary life.

Wise friends gave me journals, presumably so they would not have to listen to me bitch or would not have to visit me in prison. Orange is not my color, and a girl who eats her feelings would assuredly starve in lockup. Forgive my shameless, wicked, unhealthy thoughts. I cannot be good all the time, and truly, I have no fucking interest in being so.

Welcome to my world. If nothing else comes of this, you may feel better about your own life choices. Know that you are not alone; we all screw up. As long as we are breathing, my friend, redemption is still an option. Yes, life is a gamble, but those signs in Vegas promise both cash and redemption. I will take a double, please.

Lesson 1

JOURNAL

Journal number one was given to me by my aunt Pearl. She wrote a personal note in the front:

This book belongs to Jewel and Darrin——June 1, 1996
My dear newlyweds,

Congratulations on your bold move into the ranks of the institutionalized! Many thrive on it. Your uncle Jack and I have been married fifteen years—and they have been the best eleven years of my life! Sorry, old joke. Just realize that it took a lot of hard work to stay "in love" and "loving," but it was well worth it.

Okay——so, what is this book's purpose? Simple. It is an Anniversary Book. This year, you write in it how you met, when you knew you loved each other, when you met the parents, how you planned the wedding, and so on. Write about where you see yourselves ten years down the road, twenty, or forty! Silly stories, touching stories; things you want to remember, such as your favorite things about your wedding, your reception, and your honeymoon.

Then, every year on your anniversary, find this book, and write in it. What has happened to the two of you during the past year? What has happened in the world? How did you celebrate your anniversary? After a few years, it will be fun to pull out and read the previous years' passages. It is a once-a-year diary. My aunt and uncle have kept one of these books for forty years. They have written of

*births, deaths, promotions, demotions, men on the moon, and a dream vacation
to Ireland. It is a great gift to yourself to keep a live journal. It is not difficult.*
   God Bless!
   Aunt Pearl and Uncle John

At any point, please feel free to skip to the third lesson and look for the excla-
mation, "Seriously?" Consider this a choose-your-own-adventure book. If there
is not enough adventure in the Suzy Homemaker portion, please move ahead.
Goodness knows there was not enough adventure for me. My life did not begin
until after my marriage ended.

FEBRUARY 14, 1997

It's Valentine's Day. Darrin and I wanted some downtime after the wedding was
done and over with. Writing in this book was not a priority, so this, therefore,
is the first entry.

   I just started my own business on Monday, January 20. I resigned that same
day from ExpressTech. Darrin is incredibly supportive. He had been suggesting
the move to self-employment for quite a while.

   Tonight we will have dinner in. The restaurants will be too crowded, and
Darrin is not super social. Just in case people reading this feel they've missed
any vital wedding/honeymoon information, we have plenty of pictures. There's
a journal on the honeymoon and copious notes on the wedding for planning
purposes. We even have a copy of the ceremony as spoken by the participants. I
went nuts in order to make sure things were done right. Now, I'm going to try
to get Darrin's perspective on paper.

MAY 22, 1997

Nope, still no input from Darrin. Waiting for him could take quite some time.
We're better off being early than late for the anniversary entry. The business has
been an uphill battle. My ambition exists, but the correct personal technology
does not. My learning curve is steep, as I am not a techie. We have been trying

to build an office for me downstairs, but it's progressing slowly. We've been at it for over six months. Impatient, aren't I? This evening, I'm going to plant a butterfly bush in the yard. I hope the bush and my butterfly feeder will entice butterflies into the garden. Deer ate all my flowers, so they won't be attracting these little winged friends. Two days ago, I celebrated my twenty-fifth birthday. Erica, the daughter of my sister, Jayden, was born on May 13.

NOVEMBER 25, 1997

Today would be a good day to go over some history. Darrin and I met in July of 1992. We were both at a party at my friend Sunshine's apartment. She lived with four other girls on campus at Western Michigan University. I knew most of the people there and felt comfortable. Gay, George, Ned, and a couple of others went to high school with me. Strolling into the place, I found myself a drink and took a seat at the kitchen table to play quarters. A somewhat boring party had been ditched in the hope this would be a better one.

A mutual friend introduced us and gave us some background on each other. George especially wanted to see us argue a point together. He knew Darrin was studying to be an attorney and remembered me from political science class. George felt I could probably hold my own but wanted to pit me against Darrin.

The group also thought it was interesting that Darrin and I had each just come back from Massachusetts. Darrin gave me three numbers to reach him, which gave me some indication of his interest level. Still, he called me first. The first date was on my terms—a place close to home with loud music. In case it got boring or we had nothing to talk about, I had my escape planned.

It backfired. The conversation was interesting, and we could not hear each other speak. After dinner, we went to my parent's house and chatted on the couch. He kissed me before he left and drove away.

The second date was on Darrin's terms. I drove to my grandma's house to pick up a couch for the apartment I was planning to get. Since his father's house was in the same general direction, I called to see if he wanted a visitor. (Flint, where I was headed, is in reality almost an hour's drive from his place.)

He planned a wonderful time for us. He introduced his dad and stepmom. His brothers and sister were there, too.

We went out on the boat alone together. I wore a tiny bikini, and Darrin loved it. That may have been the decisive factor. When we brought the boat back to the dock, the family went for a ride with us. Some went tubing, but even if I'd wanted to join in with that, my top would have flown off.

Later, we had dinner at a Hungarian restaurant in Canada. After dinner, we walked to a lovely fountain and looked at the river. When we got back to his place, we sat on the couch in one of the (twenty or so) lounge areas in their house and talked.

I spent at least one night there. The trailer with which I was hauling the couch had no lights, and driving at night without them was dangerous. The Cohens had plenty of room for me at their home, and they were terrific hosts.

It's worth noting that driving into the gated community and up onto their drive felt strange. My chariot was a beat-up Delta 88 with a grandma couch jerry-rigged to the back of it. The house was (and is) a mansion perched at the edge of a large, beautiful lake. I knew it was the right place, because Darrin had told me it was somewhat big. Being something less than a multimillionaire made me feel uncomfortable in this exclusive community.

Lesson 2

LEARN FROM THE BEST

FEBRUARY 14, 1998

It's Valentine's Day once again. Darrin is at work this morning, and I'm going to run errands with my friend McKenna. This week we had a professional cook come in. She stood in our kitchen and taught the group (people who were humanistic Jews and intermarried couples) how to cook good, old-fashioned Jewish dishes. An assistant rabbi gave us ideas on how to hold a Shabbat. I for one did not know what it was until I asked.

Someone else's company has me on the payroll again. The solitude got to me. I also wasn't making the money I expected to. Now, I have my own insurance, tuition reimbursement, and vacation time. The trade-off is not bad.

Darrin and I plan to eat in this evening. No need to brave the crowds; we went out last night, anyway. My job is not far. I hope to stay there for a long time. During that time, I plan to get a master's degree in human resource administration.

Soon I will be seeing an advisor, who will give me some suggestions and help me see how difficult this program will be to work into my time and financial schedules. Within five years, I expect to have earned my higher degree, saved a large amount in my 401K, and become a valuable employee to my current company. By then, I will have put more thought into starting a family. I may even have started trying to get pregnant. We will have purchased more land and started building another house. We will be healthier than we are now, as we will be changing our eating habits and exercising more. Our two kitties will also be happy and healthy. Darrin will have moved away from the building business and further into real estate, mortgage brokering, and tax liens. He will have created more companies that I can't now even begin to imagine. I plan to start tracking my goals in order to keep on task. Soon, our income will increase, and we are trying hard to save as much as we can. At least, that's the plan.

JUNE 13, 1998

This is our official anniversary entry. I had a master's class on our anniversary, and we've been busy with other things. This evening we're trying to get things done around the house. Who am I kidding? All day we've been getting things accomplished. We were at our home away from home this morning—Home Depot. Today is closet-reorganization day.

It was also transplant day—my attempts at being a gardener. For now, though, my favorite hobby is bird-watching. It's simple, relaxing, and noncompetitive. Lately the little birdies have been hungry because the feeders have not been refilled in a couple days.

We just got back from a camping trip a little bit ago. It felt terrific to get away.

Day one of my full makeover had been scheduled this afternoon, but it unfortunately had to be rescheduled. The plan is to shop for a new outfit, get a cut and color, and have an artist apply makeup. It's all part of a gift from Paul and Cat. Sounds fun!

It was not fun.

Catherine, my evil stepmother-in-law, called me a hillbilly during the makeover at the overpriced salon in Bloomfield Hills. This was done in front of the clients and all the workers. Therefore, everyone from the shampoo girl to the receptionist to the stylists heard her insanely rude comments. Picture Joan Rivers commenting on a dress at the Oscars. We were at a shop, and she gestured to all of me, saying, "We need to get rid of *all this*." My long, blond, curly hair went—along with my personal style and all my dignity. Moreover, the result was not pretty. The look was two toned and short. The following day, we had dinner at the mansion, and she made it even worse by saying, "I spent all that money, and you still look like *this*?" Catherine is a miserable bitch. She just does not care about anything except getting high. Wake and bakes are supposed to be happy, relaxed people! Not this one—she is a monster.

FEBRUARY 21, 1999

This is our Valentine's Day entry, albeit a bit late. We've been going through the "in sickness" part of the vows this past month. Immediately following a cruise to the Mexican Riviera, I came down with a cold/flu virus that's been going around. You get a fever and a hacking cough, and you lose your appetite and hurt all over. Darrin has come down with the cold part so far. Maybe he can avoid the other stuff. Gosh, I hope so, because he is king of the man cold. Anything beyond sniffles renders him useless.

Yesterday, Dad delivered a bookcase to us. He and Mom dropped by for a couple of hours, and he will be back soon to drop off the other half of the set. They are to be built into the wall on each side of the fireplace. The stain on the oak matches all the other wood on the lower level.

The mortgage business, Sterling Financial, is coming along. We have not seen a profit yet, but expenses are being covered. My MSA program is a third of the way done, and the grades are all As so far. The workweek is fifty-five to sixty hours in addition to school, and I am proud of myself. At least, I'm proud when I steal a second to think about it.

We don't have much leisure time right now. My employer was accepting of my vacation time. For Darrin and me, spending time alone together in the sun was a positive thing. It reminded us that sometimes we truly enjoy each other's company and that we are fun to be around when we're not falling into bed after a hard day.

JULY 21, 1999

A one-week intensive class for the master's program just ended. The toughest days were when I had to go straight from the all-day to the evening course.

We are pregnant. That is a rather large event. Right now, the little person is not large. He or she is tiny. We will have the first ultrasound next month.

NOVEMBER 4, 1999

We've had three ultrasounds at this point. All the tests point to a healthy baby girl, and we are past the halfway point in the pregnancy. We're keeping a baby journal and are being good about taking "pregnant pictures" to record this stage in our lives. The next time I write, it will be a new millennium, and our lives will have changed drastically. Darrin is going to be a splendid daddy.

JUNE 5, 2000

We just celebrated our fourth anniversary. But there was not much celebration. On Thursday, the first of the month, we went to a parenting group meeting. Our beautiful baby girl screamed all day and into the night. I rushed her out of the meeting and had a good, long cry. Ella is a fussy baby. My girl is high maintenance, but we love her dearly. Her name means truth—and the truth is, she is killing me.

Ella has turned everything upside down. When she smiles, the world is right again. When she snuggles into my neck, I know I would kill for her. Sadly, those moments are rare. Right now, everything else—each piece of my existence—comes second to the baby. We know we'll have to put time and effort into our marriage. We are committed to this family.

My graduation ceremony is taking place this weekend. My goals seem to be on track. We are still in the same house but are looking for new land. I love it here and had to stop writing when someone tapped at the baby's window. It was a squirrel. I gave him a pita chip, and he was happy. Yesterday, a bunny gave himself a dirt bath outside the window downstairs.

LIFE DOES HAVE A RESET BUTTON

Flash-forward ten years into the future.

APRIL 26, 2010

*S*eriously?

Who the hell am I? *Certainly not the same one now furiously typing on her computer! Certainly not the same one who is nursing yet another breakup with a beer before noon! Not the same one who can see the bag of socks and underwear she must return to yet another man after some failed attempt at a relationship! That girl formed herself into the thing she thought her partner wanted—again! That girl was Becky Homecky.*

Becky's stories remind me of Lemony Snicket's A Series of Unfortunate Events. *You know—how they start out with a laughing elf and then tell you that is so not the way this story goes. So, you had best get to another theater if that's what you're looking for. That is my life! Add in the little Snow White birdies singing whenever I play the calm, happy nature girl. There ya go. This girl is a caricature. So, if you could just go into it knowing that little Princess Becky has no clue what life is about, you may have the patience to read without throwing up in your mouth. If not, skip the first few pages. In fact, skip to star date 10/07/2005, at least five years in. However, if you want to view her pain before she even sees it, plod slowly through.*

DECEMBER, 21, 2001

Let's see…we made it through Hanukkah, and Christmas will be here in a couple of days. If I'd thought Christmas was a busy, stress-filled season before, then doing both celebrations is absolutely crazy. Darrin was brought up Jewish before both his parents went on to marry a series of Christians. I was raised Catholic—that form of uber Christianity. I thought it would be a good idea for our daughter to experience parts of both cultures. Ella is sleeping. She's nearly two years old now. I took as much time off from the workforce as I could for my maternity leave.

After my time home was up, I worked full-time as a salaried recruiter for another temporary agency. The hours and the travels were rough. But it didn't last long. The company felt I was more committed to my family than my job and let me go. They were right—my family *is* more important. I hope that someday women will not be fired for being responsible parents. Some progressive companies do exist, but most are not. I worked for about six months after Ella turned eight months old. Now, we are home together full-time. Her vocabulary is amazing, and she is a very bright young lady. Parenting is the hardest thing I have ever done, but I'm doing it well.

JUNE 2, 2002

Darrin and I went out for sushi last night. Afterward, we browsed the Barnes & Noble bookstore. Ella stayed home with April, who is twelve and enjoys coming over to watch Ella. I've just begun potty-training Ella in earnest. Yesterday was her first day without any accidents.

Sterling Financial has just been pared down to bare bones after somehow becoming a financial drain. Darrin's new focus is on a mold-remediation company. I turned thirty last month and was not happy about it. Thirty years of age is not old, but it sure sounded like it a couple years back.

This spring we took a family cruise. My cousin Maddie came along to help with Ella. All of us had a good time. Darrin and I went on a trip together to New York City to attend his friend Joshua's wedding. It was wonderful to have a reason to be alone together, and having a chance to dress up was great. As a

SAHM (stay-at-home mom), I do not dress up much. This past year has been tough on many Americans. On September 11, a group of terrorists hijacked planes and flew them into the World Trade Center and the Pentagon. It was unexpected, and everyone was horrified. We stayed in front of our televisions and radios because we had no idea who had done this monstrous thing. Nothing akin to this has happened since, but the United States has increased its airport and border security tenfold.

JUNE 21, 2003

For our anniversary this year, I booked us a room at a bed-and-breakfast. I bought chocolates, and we picked up some champagne on the way. This was number seven for us. This past year, we began marital counseling. The first counselor was a fool. He simply could not remember names. Nor could he listen.

That was unhelpful. The next one retired and referred us to his partner, and the partner has worked out for us. We have not booked an appointment in a long time. The fact that we are not shooting hateful looks at one another is a step in the right direction. Yet I still feel ignored, overwhelmed, and underappreciated. These emotions lead to anger.

I am continuing to be a full-time SAHM. Next fall, Ella will be in pre-school. She will wear a little uniform and attend five days a week. She is three years old now, and potty training is done and over with. That was a frustrating time.

Going to the gym is part of my regular routine. It helps with weight control, and scheduling for late afternoons makes my day easier. At the end of the day, I would watch the clock, waiting for Darrin to come home. That way I could try to get a small break. But now, Ella and I go together, and she plays at the childcare center.

Ella is a remarkable kid. Her parents married each other when they were in love. This year we talked about getting divorced. Even sleeping in the same room was uncomfortable. Getting a CPAP machine helped—this is an antis-noring device for people with sleep apnea. All night, my husband would snore and keep me up. In addition, he would stop breathing. Getting the machine has allowed us to spend more time near each other. When he wears it, we both get some rest. The next project is to get him to keep the mask on while he's sleeping. When he takes it off, the ugly process starts all over again. A year ago, Darrin underwent painful surgery to stop the snoring, and while things improved slightly for a time, it did not fix the problem.

Lesson 4

ACKNOWLEDGE BOTH HIGHS AND LOWS

OCTOBER 13, 2004

Our anniversary date passed without fanfare. I got a gift certificate for a night away at a hotel. We still have not used it. Because the certificate expires soon, I asked a friend to keep Ella overnight. I babysit for friends all the time, so it was easy to ask…and hard for anyone to say no.

This year, Darrin lost almost sixty pounds. He feels better, looks better, and has more energy—and best of all, the house-shaking snoring ended. He respects himself a little more, too. I'm still holding on to about fifteen pounds I don't need. Losing them is not a priority in my life.

Ella is top priority. She enjoys her new school more than last year's school. Here, they are flexible and caring, and I always know what my kid is learning and doing. Last year's school had a "we know better than you" attitude, which annoyed me. No one knows better what his or her child needs than an active, involved parent.

High points and low points are what make life real. Our top points were the following:

* Ella's dance recital
* Acquisition of a boat

* Adoption of a dog
* Visits with family and friends
* Improvements in Darrin's health
* A new school for Ella

These were our low points:

* ED (erectile dysfunction) and our efforts to deal with it (or not)
* A lawsuit
* Issues with the dog we adopted
* Disconnection from each other
* Serious back pain

My brother, Joe, is getting married in February. He was married before, but that did not take. The wedding will be held in Jamaica. Ron, my sister's husband, filed for bankruptcy. Jayden and Ron have three biological kids and have fostered numerous children. We just visited with the family that is planning to adopt the last baby they had.

This baby's current name consists of twenty-three syllables and many vowel sounds, so we crackers dubbed him Baby J. If the paperwork goes through, he will end up placed together with his two big brothers. My sister may (or may not) have the love in her heart to adopt more children. Nevertheless, she doesn't have the time, money, or other resources to do so, and I have to doubt her motivation when the current kids seem to need more of all these things than they are getting.

OCTOBER 7, 2005

Our anniversary passed again…unnoticed and uncelebrated. This was our ninth year of marriage. It has been a bad year. I've never felt as lonely as when I am alone with my husband. My body sometimes feels like it's been crushed under a rock. Then someone comes by and sucks my soul out with a vacuum. Darrin is that soul-sucking vacuum. Unless you have a straw, no one should suck this much.

My darling husband gained half his weight back, just enough of it around his neck to make the snoring return. But the CPAP machine has been collecting dust in storage. He will not wear it. It doesn't matter. I stopped giving my life and my heart when I noticed I was getting nothing in return. My husband gives 90 percent to his business, and the other 10 percent is distributed everywhere else. That is hurtful. It's hurtful that someone I loved threw away a chance at a good relationship with his wife and daughter. It's beyond me how money can seduce people into ignoring what is real. It's also beyond me how he can sleep so soundly after fleecing so many innocent victims. Okay—well, he really sleeps with a *lot* of sound, but he's able to sleep under conditions where my conscience would keep me up at night. Instead, he sleeps like a baby. If someone I loved was in pain, or if I'd caused that much pain, it would be hard for me to sleep.

AUGUST 6, 2007

Darrin and I finalized our divorce this winter. We stopped celebrating our anniversary years ago. There just was not anything to celebrate. The covenant was broken. No one cheated; we just quit. Final responsibility for serving the papers was mine.

Back in 2003, when we first broached the subject of divorce, Darrin told me he would take everything if I left him. The discussion did not lead into what we could do to make things right. The discussion was about who had ownership of my life. The gilding on the cage was never as pretty after that day in the winter of 2003.

In July 2005, a server came to the house and dropped off the papers. We were all home. When he went to the door, Darrin remarked, "I wonder who's suing me this time?" Then he read the first sheet and said, "Oh, it's my wife."

For six months, until the papers were done, we lived in the same house. That's to be expected when a minor child is involved. It was painful and strange, but everyone survived.

It has been over two years since the journey through divorce began. It was a devastating experience. The pain is similar to the pain of childbirth. Comparable to childbirth, a woman does not know how she is going to survive it, but she knows she will. My own rebirth has been similar to that.

The lessons learned are tough, but I will teach them to my own daughter. We will honor the truth. Laura Ingalls Wilder once wrote, "I am beginning to learn that it is the sweet, simple things in life that are the real ones after all." My wish for Ella is that she one day understands that love, honor, and joy make up the foundation of a healthy relationship. Without these things, you can become what I ended up being: empty. Giving everything you have to someone who always wants more is soul crushing.

What kept me going were my friends. Being married to a lawyer, I didn't write a whole lot down. In retrospect, that was probably best, as what you say can and will be used against you.

NOVEMBER 27, 2007

Heading over to Walnut Grove, Michigan, for Thanksgiving was relaxing. Ella had a wonderful time with her cousins. My sister's foster baby can't talk yet, and he is almost two. My sister tells me that's common for crack babies. Fetal alcohol syndrome leads to a lack of conscience, but that does not excuse anyone from trying to fix the problem. My ex's mom is a big drinker, but that doesn't mean Darrin gets to continue his life of crime without consequence. It's a blessing the child (little Rhett) cannot speak, because one day he'll tell the social workers they call him Niglet. Pretty sure they would frown on that one—even in Walnut Grove.

I do have a boyfriend, and things are good. We've been together about a year now. He was all meaningful and stuff last night, so I had to start making a production of doing shots. Emotional intimacy is not my strong suit. Drinking is my strong suit. Nice.

NOVEMBER 28, 2007

I am completely appalled by the nasty little names used on my nephew. I am not the classiest girl, but kids are kids, and that shit is just wrong. No one should be that hateful to anyone. People's skin color is no reason, people's religion is no reason—there just is no reason. Moreover, no one should ever be that way to a tiny being that he or she has sworn to protect. If this kid turns out okay, it will be a miracle.

The boyfriend thing is good. He has been supportive and loving. This means he earned a real name. Jackson, also known as Jax, for short, is doing more household repairs, too.

NOVEMBER 29, 2007

So, I'm pushing for feedback on all my interviews, and the response from one company was that the controller pulled in someone he had worked with in the past. Damn it! So, now I'm in line for a temporary call-center job in Troy. In addition, I'm waiting to have a second and third interview arranged at a place in Bloomfield Hills for a position as an accounting assistant. My friends had to push my résumé to the front of the stack for those jobs, and they barely break $20,000 a year. No wonder there are so many foreclosures.

Lesson 5

LEARN TO RECOGNIZE FUCKTARDS

NOVEMBER 30, 2007

Darrin has already called this morning with a parenting issue. Last week they left her glasses in a dressing room at the mall. This morning they couldn't find her winter coat, so he asked me to bring an extra to school. I explained that I don't have extra winter coats and boots.

Last night, the question was, "What might little children want for the holidays?" He was thinking books and CDs—for the under-two set. I suggested—pleasantly—that they could grow into them and suggested clothes and teddy bears for now.

DECEMBER 4, 2007

At my last family wedding, the groomsmen wore camouflage. Oh, it's true. In addition, we had a groom's cake in the shape of a deer head. The camouflage might top the Big Bites and Slurpees at the Baptist church gymnasium a few years back. That first marriage, with the reception in the gym, didn't last, so whatever money was spent was wasted anyway.

During my stroll down memory lane today, I watched DVDs of Ella growing up. Yup, and wrote out all my Christmas cards. Next big project: scrapbooking.

Dude, little sister here is getting a tad obsessive. Someone hand me a bottle of Paxil and a bottle of Jack, and it'll all be fine.

DECEMBER 11, 2007

I am now gainfully employed in a professional position completed with insurance, 401K, and paid time off. There is no beer machine, and no copies of *Juggs* magazine litter the shitter, but I think I can adapt. The hours are eight to five, and I am an administrative assistant.

DECEMBER 19, 2007
CHRISTMAS IS UPON US.

My prayers are with McKenna and her mother. Family is such a complicated thing. I can't even begin to comprehend all the emotions she must be feeling. I have no advice, only sympathy. Her mom is in a nursing home in another state and becoming increasingly ill.

Every day, at work, I have numerous new training sessions at the office on "how and where we file and find things in our paperless system." The company saves a lot of money by having an administrative staff do 80 percent of the paperwork. Imagine sending all your tasks to an admin pool and having them done for you. Dude, I need an admin pool at my house.

Jax, the boyfriend, is still entertaining hopes that I will attend the Christmas Eve party at his ex-wife's house. I'm positive I was not unclear on my feelings, and those feelings were clearly not positive.

The backstory is that my boyfriend planned to be with me on Christmas Eve. Then he called to say that he was spending Christmas Eve at the ex's home with his family and that I was, of course, invited. Mighty white of him. Far be it from me to overreact. The next day, I called to say I had changed my evening plans…and *any* plans with him until further notice. This call was made while at the mall using his credit card. New man, or new jewelry? Why not both?

DECEMBER 29, 2007
GRATEFULNESS

Okay, I'm back in the mix and trying to get used to my new schedule. Good thing it's not a bad schedule. I work eight to five with an hour for lunch. My job is close to home, and the dress code is business casual. I am so pleased to be working.

SHOP TALK

Work was frustrating at first because no one felt they had time to train me. The tasks I am given are seriously complicated, a bit arbitrary, and not necessarily logical. Therefore, I am repeatedly getting shit from my boss for not doing something I had no idea even existed or was my responsibility. I'm the new girl, so everyone gave me their shit work and said it needed to be done ASAP. In this case, management noticed and did something about it. My HR person held my hand and said, "Here is what we think is happening. You are being set up to fail, we believe in your worth to our organization, and here is how we propose to fix it." Score one for management. The HR lady has been out sick with the flu. Nevertheless, she's still checking in to make sure I'm all right. As long as someone's in my corner, I have a chance at success.

CHRISTMASES PAST, PRESENT, AND FUTURE

Um…yeah, regarding the Christmas Eve debacle…I came out all right on that one.

There was the shopping spree, the important discussions of minimum requirements, and my refusal to schedule anything holiday related. Don't worry; I scare myself, too.

FAMILY

The weekend before Christmas, I went to my mom and dad's place. During that jaunt, we went in the car with them to Davison for a large family function.

We sang carols and listened to stories about how Christmas used to be when they were kids. Then we saw my mom's side of the family, and they opened gifts and told stories. I chased the kids around and played with them, because to me, Christmas is about kids. Then we left without Ella's Girl Scout cookie order form. They found it last night in a search-and-rescue mission in Durand, Michigan, and will mail it to me. My father made woodcrafts for all the children who were not mine. That was shitty, but par for the course. I suggested presenting those gifts later without her knowledge so that the exclusion would not be so obvious.

FAMILY AND EX-FAMILY

Ella and I got back in time to drop her off at her daddy's office on the afternoon of Christmas Eve. Then, in honor of my ex, as he is the devil, I made more deviled eggs for another party and hung out with Stacey and some of my girls. Anyway, Jax had told me that he would be at my home, as originally planned, at eight thirty. To use Jewel-speak, he said something like, "Do what you will with that information, but this is where I will be." Of course, I considered making him wait because...well, just because.

PRESENTS AND FUTURE

I gave Jax his present, purchased by the two of us with his credit card. Classy. Afterward, I opened a bunch of lovely boxes containing fun, cute, and sweet things. The last box held a ring—a diamonds-and-sapphires channel set in white gold. Apparently my speech about putting the past behind you and moving on with your life was highly effective (and I must be much more intimidating than I look). For the record, "friendship ring" is the official label on this because I cannot picture myself "enGAGed." To him it signifies his long-term intention, which is forever. Jax eloquently described his feelings, what I mean to him, and how proud he is to have me in his life.

He spent the night here (yes, I am sparing details) while Ella was at Darrin's. Then we split up to be with our kids and exes for the morning. Afterward, Jack brought his kids over for dinner with Ella and me. We exchanged all the gifts he'd bought for us to give to each other. I am very generous to his children. No wonder he works seven days a week; he's taking good care of all of us.

JANUARY 13, 2008

I'm pleased to be able to report that people have come over to my side at the job. Now, we have a new situation. The human resources administrator is leaving for a new position. She is a good chick, once divorced, a biker, and a straight shooter. This was all in her master plan, and she sees this as a significant opportunity for me. No wonder she said, "You don't intimidate me" when I first walked into the room to be interviewed. Yes, I should question why anyone would feel the need to tell an interviewee that.

Lesson 6

ACCEPT IMPERFECTIONS

JANUARY 27, 2008

My Ella is a nose breather. That just means she has to work harder to eat like a human. We are finally past the "put the tarp down—Ella is coming to the table" stage. That was scary. She simply does not pay any attention when she eats. I'm constantly taking my hand and closing my fingers slowly to remind her to chew with her mouth closed. Darrin doesn't notice. His table manners are impeccable, but he doesn't really notice other people.

Speaking of meals, last night Jax took Darrin, Ella, and me out to dinner. Darrin had asked to come by and get sleds from my place on his way to the sledding hill. Then he asked if I cared to join them. I accepted, and we all played in the snow. Jax passed us on his way to my place from work and stopped by the bar/restaurant to watch the game. After sledding, he didn't think anyone would feel like going home and cooking, so he suggested we eat out. He was shocked when Darrin accepted his invitation to join us. The two have met numerous times during pickups and drop-offs. When threw a Halloween party, both were invited. But this was the first time we were all at a small table together. It was...interesting.

Darrin ordered a Cobb salad and a hot toddy. Darrin acts like a ninety-year-old geezer; Jax was the one running up and down the hill with Ella while we were sledding. Surprising, because Jax is old enough to be my father, and yet I struggle to keep up with him. Darrin is the father of my child, and your grandpa could beat him in a footrace.

The Star of David that Ella wears every day was a gift from Jax last year. She loves it. I think she appreciates the idea of being a little different. I was surprised I felt so strongly about her being regarded as Jewish. She is often called "the little Jewish girl." Her friend's teacher assumed her parents were both Jewish.

As it turns out, my kid thought I *was* Jewish. Granted, my nickname is Jew (short for Jewel), and I do know a few prayers, recipes, a little Yiddish, and some cultural tidbits. But I do not self-identify that way. We celebrate those holidays out of respect to that part of her heritage. She asked me to continue with the tradition after the divorce, and guilt is a powerful motivator in both Jewish and Catholic cultures.

Ella was in a temple one time, with me, for her great-grandmother's funeral. We both enjoy attending church but have simply gotten out of the habit. We would go with a group of people, and as they dropped out, it became easier to do the same thing. Therefore, yes—I am planning to start going again. Hanukkah is the only Jewish holiday I celebrate with Ella. The rest of the year, we don't do anything, and Hanukkah is just the way to compete with Christmas. It's actually a minor holiday in Israel. She asked about a bat mitzvah, and I told her that her dad is the one to address on this issue. I was thinking that a cross necklace coming from Grandma would be less obvious than from me, and it would be easy for Grandma's gift to trump Jack's.

Ella is at Darrin's, Jack is at work, and I have brunch planned with some girlfriends. The elementary school homework is obnoxious, and my kid fusses more than studies. She has writing assignments, reading assignments, and math assignments. She has special projects, too. She used to read twenty minutes per day, but now we have only about an hour between the time I pick her up and bedtime. I make dinner, eat with her, talk about our day and our week, and then I clean up. As I'm cleaning up, she's getting ready for bed. Homework is mostly for weekends or if we have time in the morning.

FEBRUARY 1, 2008

I am planning a trip…and excited about doing girl shit. How did I become this person who shovels snow, cooks squirrel (just kidding), does dishes, cleans her house, does homework with her kid, washes loads of laundry, teaches good manners, sells girl scout cookies, and goes to jewelry parties? WTF! When did I suddenly become an adult? I hate it sometimes. No one should spend half her life in the kitchen. I need to be spoiled.

FEBRUARY 4, 2008

When Jax came out to my place Sunday night, I was surprised. What kind of guy leaves the bar during the Super Bowl and ditches the dudes to be with some girl at halftime? I asked him what kind of shit he had to take for that one. Mr. Smooth said, "They know you. They get it. They wish they were me." So, I go for the zipper and…no, seriously, he was more interested in keeping score for the squares. I married a square, and I'm done with that shit. Oh, and I had no money on it, truth be told. Last year, we watched from room 318 at the Holiday Inn Express.

FEBRUARY 10, 2008

This weekend, I played supermom as opposed to bitchy, grumpy, or hungover mom. Yup, one stinking degree outside, and *I am at Kroger, selling Girl Scout c-c-cookies.* Just to make it even better, *we were not inside the store.* Of course not. We were between the doors. The doors froze shut, that's how freakin' cold it was. Shoppers were spending a lot of time staring at the doors, so much so that I put up a sign, because the retards at Kroger didn't think to do it. It was the only thing that made sense to me. Then I was accused of breaking the doors because it was too cold. That did not go over well. I went into my "speak slowly to the stupid people" mode. In addition, I watched obnoxious kid movies, baked and frosted cookies, and played kid games. That should last me until spring, right?

FEBRUARY 12, 2008

They let us out of work a little early, and that saved me an hour's worth of drive time, minimum. At least it would have if my babysitter had been at her house with my kid. I called to alert her, but this may be the last person on earth without a mobile phone. She's also the second-to-worst driver on God's green earth—the worst being my ex-mom-in-law. Now, I'm annoyed that I must hunt down my child later in the evening when all I want to do is stay in and stay warm and safe. More importantly, I question how my child is going to make it back in one piece. On a perfect, sunny summer day, this one could go slipping and sliding down the road. I drove to her house, hoping they maybe just weren't able to come to the phone. That would be a better option than saying, "Hey, there's a blizzard coming. Here's an idea—let's drive all over creation and go paint plaster, because we certainly cannot paint plaster at any of the ten places we're going to pass on the way there. Then we'll leave late and not give ourselves enough time to get home, and we can have a back seat full of grumpy kids ready to kill each other...that is, if the other drivers don't kill us first."

FEBRUARY 18, 2008

Reservations were made at the Holiday Inn this weekend. It was delightful. This was our late Valentine's Day celebration. Mac can attest to the fact that the boyfriend is not slacking (LOWES). The whole minimum requirement speech does not have to be repeated often. Everyone should have a minimum requirements list. This is how we know what we are willing to accept. When those minimum expectations go unmet, that list becomes a speech. No one wants to be the recipient of a minimum requirements speech, because it means trouble.

We got a suite with a Jacuzzi tub and picked up food to feed each other in bed. I had champagne and orange juice in the morning, savoring the late checkout time of two o'clock. Now, I finally feel relaxed. It's been months since Jackson and I just lay around. He works long days, and that equates to almost no time together in daylight hours. I was starting to feel married. Poor guy actually says, "Would that be so bad?" The answer is a resounding *yes!* That would be so bad. That was so bad. The next contestant on *The Bitch Is Right* will have to go through one hell of a test run.

Anyway, it was tremendous to relax and just *be*. Okay, and be *done*. This was the first weekend we rented a movie. Other relationships are not like this one.

It works, but it's definitely different from what I expected. We talk for hours. That is *so* not reminiscent of life with my ex, the cheap ass rat bastard, CARB, for short.. He was a mute in comparison. This is fantastic. But I miss the little perks (plays and vacations and expensive jewelry). I own that. However, the tradeoff is much more satisfying. Now, if Jack could just win the lotto…

The job is all right. However, the pregnant chick keeps retching in front of me. Moe, Mac's boyfriend, would throw up if he had to see this…and hear it. He is a friendly puker. She, on the other hand, was carrying a trashcan and puking all the way to the bathroom. My desk is on the way there, so I get to see this every half hour or so. Aren't partial-birth abortions still legal? She might wanna consider. I'd throw in a coupla bucks. She is about six months in, and there is nothing wrong with pregnancy. I just dislike this girl because she is dirty. She's dirty—just…dirty.

MARCH 5, 2008

This morning was unreal. The snow must end. Jack did the driveway this morning and hacked away at the ice last night. He has been very, very good lately. I took care of him when he got the flu, so now I have hit goddess status. I thought I'd hit the lottery when I married a guy whose mother couldn't cook. No way. That was nothin'. Now I find a guy who hated to come home to his wife's complaining every night. I offer him a shot and a beer occasionally, and he is enamored. Picture me hitting the easy button. My life is not so incredibly difficult.

Lesson 7

FUCK IT—CELEBRATE IMPERFECTIONS!

MARCH 12, 2008

Let me tell you about the fiasco at Ella's birthday party at Lakeland School, where Darrin's pants were stolen. The pants themselves were not important to me. The fact that the pants held his keys and *my only set of keys* plus a wallet and cell phone was troublesome. Because of this, I needed to find a ride home for myself, my child, and my parents, who'd come in from out of town. Darrin, in his cold, wet swimsuit, bummed a ride from Denise. I had no choice but to leave my car overnight in the lot at the pool where the party had been held until I could get to an open dealership. Moreover, I was concerned that people who steal might decide to take the car and everything in it. Why not? Obviously, their morals were lacking. Inside the car were all of Ella's gifts, her treats for school the next day, my mother's purse, and our coats. The car was not stolen, thank goodness, but it put a damper on the party mood nonetheless. My locks have *still* not been replaced. Darrin did look miserable in his cold, wet swimsuit. That was one bit of joy.

It's good to have my friend Gayle back from Korea. She lives in Bloomfield now, and she and her daughter made it to the birthday party.

The pregnant chick finally just stopped showing up to work altogether. She has always been dirty. Now she's poor and dirty *and* knocked up with some child. Her nickname is the Dirty Mexican. The filthy blanket she wraps around herself makes it look like all she's missing is the sombrero. Instead of hiring someone else, the company demoted Frances, who is a bright young woman with a master's in IT, and put her at my level. Nice. Frances had no choice but to take the sucky offer. Frances is also pregnant, but she is not dirty.

My sister is currently housing seven children: her own three; two new foster kids; one old foster child, Rhett (a.k.a. Giblet, Niglet, Jigaboo); and a little boy in her new day care paid for by the state. I know the extra little boy's mom from Walnut Grove. Back in the day, she was just a buggy-eyed girl with stringy hair and a big self-esteem problem. Seems she has graduated to alcoholic welfare mom. In addition, she has so limited her options that she can only get my sister as a caregiver. That is skid row.

My friend Lainie calls with updates of her sexcapades. She's recently divorced and getting all the action she can. Her new boy toy makes her feel sexy, and that's especially helpful after her mastectomy and the divorce her husband asked for when he changed his mind about the sickness part of the contract. Go, Lainie! She and I met in geology class and she is one of the few college buddies I am still dear friends with.

My dear friends must promise *never* to let me walk around with a mustache or beard. Holy cow, I have seen so many women with copious hair on their faces lately. I'm going to start carrying sheep-shearing scissors around in my purse. At Sam's Club, the chick behind the counter should have been wearing one of those things to cover facial hair. We can't all be divas, but we need to follow at least the minimum requirements. In fact, if I'm in a coma, one of the bitches needs to make sure I don't have embarrassing crud happening with my face. No ogre hairs are allowed.

MARCH 19, 2008

Jackson and I are going to see the sun. We are headed to Altamonte Springs (Orlando) in Florida. We leave on Friday night and are coming back on Wednesday. The chilluns are going on vacations, and we're doing the romantic-getaway thing. Wanna hear reason number 50,689 why I am the perfect girlfriend? Before we went out to celebrate St. Paddy's Day, we were spending quality time—well, he was spending quality time—down there… and I say, "Damn, why do we even talk?" Nice fucking friends. I was seriously annoyed that I'd wasted time having meaningful conversation. What kinda wrong is that? Why do they have pictures of stupid enGAGment rings on my computer screen? Someone must show me how to get rid of them. And why don't the random voices in my head just *shut up*?

Maybe I really do need that vacation, huh, girls. Dude put me on as beneficiary for his 401K. Wow, that's much better than bumming money for smokes like Sam, AKA, Scammy VanMeter, one of my ex boyfriends, used to do. The Cohens use insurance fraud as an income enhancer. How funny that I work for people who catch people who defraud like Darrin and make them pay up. It's called subrogation, and we work mostly with insurance companies.

Jack's other nickname, Soldier Boy, has a story behind it. My boyfriend told me he was in Nam. Now, dude is old, but the people who went to Vietnam are usually older. His story is that he went there as a marine. The war was officially supposed to be over, but the United States did not get out and were still sending in troops. To this day, he refuses to stay in a tent, because he spent too much time in tents in the jungles of Vietnam. That means no camping for us. His time there also left him with posttraumatic stress disorder. This is supposedly why he self-medicates.

MARCH 31, 2008

So, I barely got out of town on Friday. I did not take the day off work because I was conserving my paid time off. I waited until late in the day to see if they would let us out a little early. The clock *tick, tick, ticked* along, and the snow advisories kept coming. So, I decided to take off an hour early. Just as I was preparing to go, they let us out early.

I passed eleven accidents on the way to Detroit Metropolitan Airport, one of them making Jax and I back up and find another route. We were on the tarmac for over two hours and did not get to our hotel until about four in the morning. Ouch. Still, we found the energy to bust the headboard. Earlier in the week, I'd developed some sort of respiratory issue that caused a nasty cough and strange croaking noises to come out of my mouth when I spoke.

Uncool. I sucked cough drops like mad so that I would not be drawn and quartered for being the bubonic plague bitch. Typhoid Mary was a cook who knew she had it but needed the work. The following day, we bought cough syrup. Delsym is good stuff. It worked well and even seemed to help with the aches. Now, it should have lasted more than a day. That's why people use measuring spoons instead of slugging it like I did! On Sunday, I asked the pharmacy for a spoon and picked up a new bottle.

Most nights, I was ready to pass out by ten. Thankfully, my dude was just happy to have me in bed next to him. We lay by the pool, but it was a little cold to swim. We watched movies in our room and walked to dinner one night. We went for drives and walked along the beach. We hit the hotel bar and slow danced. Yes, we were the only people dancing. I went to Gatorland to get my friend Stacey a T-shirt. Speaking of T-shirts, guess what shirt I found in children's sizes? Yep…and I got one in pink for Ella. Okay, maybe not. When I went to New Orleans, years ago, I asked if they had "Fuck You, You Fucking Fuck" shirts in children's sizes. They did not. However, you can get them specially made in Old Town, Florida.

This afternoon, at work, I was told that I'd made a mistake and that we are a small company that cannot afford mistakes. I do make mistakes, and the more people's jobs I take on, the more mistakes I'm going to make. In this case, a claim number had been listed in a document in a few different formats. I chose the most common format, as all my actions are timed exercises, each keystroke documented and put into a spreadsheet. This was mathematically and logically sound, but it wasn't the right answer in this case. Does this mean I'm not going to win the Data Entry Clerk of the Year Award? Yes, that…*and I am fired.* On the drive home, I was dreading walking in and telling my daughter. Nice. The good news is that my career is the only thing that is *not* going well in my life. Everything else except work is in working order.

APRIL 1, 2008

I would have stayed in Sucksville as long as I could until something better came along. But in truth, I wasn't trying to find anything better because I had given up on the idea of a rewarding career. I'd settled for the ability to pay (part of) the bills. Searching for a job is depressing, and let me be the first to say that *I ought to know.*

Yes, Ella recommended that I apply to McDonald's again. I have not found my niche, and maybe now I can take some time and *not* take the first thing that comes along. For example, at Weight Loss Giant, a possible class-action lawsuit is pending for consistently breaking federal employment laws. At another place, the paychecks bounced, and the boss was a bit of a sleazeball.

All jokes aside, I need to take responsibility. I'm in my late thirties with no working plan for the future, and now I have a spotty employment record. The good news is that I did not do anything to embarrass my friend Eve, who recommended me to the company. Last week, they asked a part timer, an eighteen-year-old, to go full-time without offering her benefits. She lives at home and just got her driver's license. Budget-wise, this made sense to the firm. They've dropped three people since I arrived and hired one. This is where we live. If I can prove that I add enough value to a company, they will do what it takes to keep me. The kid's data-entry skills outpace my own. My typing speed is thirty-five words per minute. One of my important duties was to add paper to the printers. That will go on my résumé, for sure.

The budget crunch, at the office, is real. I was denied permission to order any coffee, cream, cups, copy paper, or toner. Yes, we ran out of every single one of these things—go figure. However, they did have the money to spend on hundreds of little plastic flashing ice cubes for a sales conference at a dollar a pop.

It's hard—very hard—to admit that I'm back to where I was a year ago, even two years ago. But it's my life, and only I can change it. We all know from experience that our health, our friends, and our family are what count in this world.

Being hateful is useless. The house had to go up for sale anyway, and this wasn't the best job fit. The car can go back this summer, and unemployment will cover the grocery bill. I found a food pantry that I qualify for already, and Jack's hours will increase soon. He'll help when he can. In addition, I got my tax refund back. Once again, thank goodness for alimony. I told Darrin, and he offered to help; he seemed genuinely concerned. Jax doesn't know yet, but I'll tell him when I see him tonight. I'm not keeping it from him, but it's not a pleasant voice-mail message when you can't get the real deal.

This morning I'm revising the résumé and trying to come up with some short-term plans. I am not a loser; I just keep playing the wrong games.

Lesson 8

REMEMBER YOUR ROOTS

J ournal number two was a gift from McKenna, and she wrote an inscription
to me on the inside cover:

This journal belongs to Jewel Cohen
The best time to journal is when you're facing difficult times—you'll be able to
look back later and see how strong you really are.

If the first journal was dedicated to my marriage, the second is a testament to
my recovery from that soul-sucking arrangement. The goal is to move from
bitter to better.

APRIL 7, 2008

It's Monday morning. The sun is out, and the birds are singing. Yesterday I
went for a walk and heard a chorus of spring peepers. Spring is about new
beginnings.

This journal may also be about new beginnings. I will write freely and let
it be what it will be.

This morning I'm drinking coffee and eating oatmeal while waiting for
Darrin and Ella to drop by. He said he doesn't have a coat for her. He does. The

coat at his house is pretty—it has patchwork brocade, velvet, and fake fur. He just didn't bother to look for it.

That is my ex in a nutshell. If he cannot see it, it does not exist. This, of course, includes feelings. And…this is why we are not soul mates. For us to be soul mates, the man would need to have a soul. That must have been why he wanted mine.

Now, that just seems mean. It wasn't so much his lack of soul as his lack of conscience. Have you ever met a person who is only happy when he or she has the upper hand? I have, and I married one of them. Yeah. Go, me.

When we look back, most of our mistakes are preventable. Here's a prime example. When I met my ex, he was cheating at quarters. Yup, the game where there are no clear-cut winners but everyone stumbles away happy. He cheated.

APRIL 10, 2008

Sarcasm is used to deal with latent anger. If words are a tool, then sarcasm is my sharpest weapon. My old boyfriend Aiden once accused me of being an angry person. Aiden—what a cutie. He was a sweet, pretty little boy. He should have been the one who was angry.

His daddy was full-blooded Irish, and they lived in Dorchester, Massachusetts, in a tiny flat. My honey got the crap kicked out of him on a regular basis by his raging alcoholic pop. Aiden could have been all kinds of ugly. Instead, my Aiden was an angel.

Aiden was my best friend when I left my raging asshole boyfriend. Leaving a guy is easy. I should know. Sticking with them is my sticking point. Aiden may have gotten the impression that I had anger-management issues when I told him he had a tiny, useless penis. If you're out there, Aiden, I lied. I was angry. I guess you were right about me.

Same day, later in the evening…

I got up early and prepped for the morning routine. There was a page of math homework waiting for Ella, and breakfast consisted of toasted bagels and cream cheese. She was ready, and we were running early. We had time to talk and mess with her hair. Most prep is done the night before to avoid hassle.

My plan today was to do some outside spring cleaning, like raking. Instead, after my kid was dropped off, my girlfriend called and suggested coffee. I told her I had a pot brewing at my place and some errands to run later if she wanted to join me.

Being frugal is not a choice but a necessity—my coffee is served in-house. When I'm gainfully employed, my coffee is enjoyed at work. The cheapness might have rubbed off on me.

Gainfully employed—there's a term for you. Not sure I've *ever* been gainfully employed. Employed, yes—many, many times. A different employer for every year I've been on this earth. My mother is so proud.

The good news is that there are jobs. The bad news is that they are the jobs that nobody wants and nobody stays in. Here are one or two examples.

Today I went to the district court to file nonperiodic garnishment papers on a former employer's bank account. This employer said he could not afford to pay me—after he was into me for two weeks' pay. It gets worse. To prevent myself from getting boned on the deal, I suggested he cut me a deal on a home-improvement project. The company did hardwood flooring, and mine was in need of a touch-up.

His hillbilly, crack-smoking employees destroyed my floors. No wonder the business was going under! When I gave my whole "this is completely unacceptable" speech, the workers never returned. So, I was left with all my furniture pushed into other rooms, sitting outside, or stacked in my lower level. My walls were nicked, my paint was chipped, and they sanded part of a room that was not on the estimate. Shoe molding? Nope, not that, either.

To fix everything and bring a mover in for the furniture could have cost up to five grand. I would have been hard pressed to come up with fifty dollars. So, I fixed what I could with the help of Stacey and asked my neighbor for help with two large items—a month or so later. You see...

A painter had been hired, but he quit showing up. He was paid cash each time he came. He rode his bike. For future reference, do not hire painters who ride bicycles; they may be less than dependable. Perhaps my next book will be a home-improvement guide. This is just a tiny excerpt. Also, please refrain from hiring contractors who have beer machines on premises. Oh, yeah...that goes right along with asking the following questions: Are you a member of the Better Business Bureau? Do you have a license? Do you have workers' compensation and liability insurance? Who are five people I can call as references?

Back to the painter on the bicycle...yeah, that was my employer's cousin. The painter was a decent kid but not very motivated. It's just painting, right? He hired an immigrant to come and do the hard stuff. You know you're overpaying when they subcontract it out to another ethnic group.

The kid just kinda fell off the face of the earth. I tracked down his mom to see if I could get my house key back. I would have come to pick it up, or it could be dropped in the mail. Nope, the kid still has it. All I could do was pray that he lost it and didn't give it to his shifty, perverted uncle.

This meant the whole first level of my home was completely devoid of furniture, all the window treatments were down, and painters' tape was up everywhere—thanks to the Mexican hired by the kid, who lives at home with his mother.

The good news is that being unemployed gives me time to spackle and paint. The bad news is that I have no experience. In addition, I have the Epstein-Barr virus in the form of mono—the kissing disease. No wonder I resemble the walking dead and the wracking cough will not go away.

Back up a little, and get the full picture. I have bronchitis, and I worked for a company that sands floors. Oh, yeah...and when the employees are not smoking crack, they smoke cigarettes. Moreover, as I'm doing the books and watching the company sink deeper into financial ruin, my boss plans a new office-improvement project that comes complete with an extra inch of dust on my desk. The surgical mask and goggles I donned as a hint that we might want to do this office-improvement project after hours was not a big enough hint.

Okay, so I was obviously undervalued as an employee and as a person. Somehow seeing the *Juggs* magazines in the bathroom and the porn downloaded onto all the computers did not tip me off to this fact. As office manager, one of my duties was to read and respond to e-mails. How the heck are you supposed to respond to pornographic e-mails? The worst offenders were easily recognized and their messages avoided.

However, some were difficult to ignore. My boss's daughter was receiving e-mails from men in their thirties. His daughter was barely twelve! She signed on to a dating site with her cousin. That needed to be addressed before little Lily was *undressed* by a toothless pedophile. Well, sure, I looked at the photos. I was single—sort of.

APRIL 11, 2008

Last night, sleep would not come. Coffee is to blame. I only drank it in the morning, but someone or something must take the blame. We cannot blame joblessness, because that is a normal state of being in my state. Michigan heads the nation in joblessness and foreclosures. Somehow being part of a greater trend doesn't help the sleeplessness.

For the majority of my life, unemployment was a nonissue. I lived at home and then lived away at college and then lived with my fiancé. See, there was always a plan. There were always jobs. While I lived at my parent's house, I had kids to babysit, a clerical school co-op job, and a local ice-cream store that needed tending.

The ice-cream store was the most fun. Yes, we could eat anything we sold and then some. If it was in the place and was edible, it was mine. My friend, Madge, and I came up with some crazy sundae flavors. Hey, we didn't know it was guacamole.

This was small-town living. Walnut Grove had no stoplight. The library was the size of a one-room schoolhouse, and the museum was the size of a shed. In the town square, there was a park and a small theater aptly titled the Park Theatre. We saw movies like *Herbie, the Love Bug* there.

Ah, small-town life has its characters. The drug dealer who was also a gigolo paid in hundred-dollar bills to see if my eyes would light up. The junk dealer would come by for coffee and leave tips. A lovely couple who also owned the antique store next door owned the ice-cream shop. In addition, they sold bait. Yes, people did order ice cream and live bait, and I had the privilege of serving them both. That was my first taxpaying job. It paid $3.25 an hour, which was minimum wage at the time.

By the way, no one I knew hung out with the jacked-up gigolo, whose name was Jack. However, there was a suitor who came by the ice-cream stand—the infamous guy with the butt-purse fanny pack. Gigolo Jack might have been a better choice.

APRIL 13, 2008

Sunday morning. I'm at the kitchen table, and my man is doing dishes. Life is good. He's got no shirt on, and I'd be so excited…but the slippers take away the hotness factor just a little. We'll have to kick it up a notch with a little Sunday-morning porn. That'll get me there. Heck, maybe I'll even whip my own slippers off.

Last night we were at a hot-tub party, and this morning I threw away a Taco Bell receipt time-stamped 2:36 a.m. The fact that we can stay up that late is impressive. I think I'll dig it out of the trash and frame it.

Lesson 9

COME BACK WITH YOUR SHIELD—OR *ON* IT

APRIL 14, 2008

So, the Fake Jew is considering taking Ella to temple—at her request. She thinks she wants a bat mitzvah. Stop the insanity! Darrin has mixed feelings because he does not know a damn thing about Judaism, and it costs money to attend a temple not to mention throw a bat mitzvah. I say own it, dude. Just tell her it's a farce! You are and have always been a fraud. Yes, he knows the dictionary definition of the word because *he lost a fraud case in court*. Thank goodness bitterness is not a part of my being.

Remember how I weaseled my way into getting a cross around Ella's neck? In short, I bought one with Jack's credit card and gave it to Jack's daughter to give to Ella. So, she wears it all of two days, and it mysteriously disappears. I called Darrin out on it. He said he took it off for her bath because it might not be able to take the water. Translation: "Your dude probably gave her cheap shit." He never removed the Star of David necklace Jack bought her. I never remove the promise/friendship ring Jack bought me. Nope, doesn't fly. So, he said he would send it back in a baggie. It never came back. I went to his house and retrieved it. Then I put it on myself. Why? Because I need to prove that I am Christian! Guh! Being supportive was such a bad idea! That must stop. I am a recovering Catholic and proud of it. Uh…that didn't come out right.

I'm now waiting to see how this plays out. My guess is that she will sense Daddy's wild discomfort and feel bad about going. If not, they have my permission to get involved in any religious training he feels will be beneficial. Darrin was hoping I would be the bad guy. No way. He's not getting out of this with a free pass. I said he could take her to temple to study any night of the week. In addition, I'm willing to let him pick her up from my home and take her to temple every Saturday we are in town. This man will have every bit of rope he needs. Maybe he'll meet someone similar to himself (grandmotherly) and live unhappily ever after. Whatever happens, my child will not be the first real Jew in three generations.

APRIL 15, 2008

Some people are bad at making doctor's appointments. I am one of those people. People do this for a number of reasons. For me, the best way is a visual. Right now, my butt is sitting in an area McDonald's. I'm early but want to spend as little time in the doctor's waiting room as possible. My feet are resting on the balls of my heels, toes up. I do this when anxious, and anxiety is a part of me. Come to think of it, nothing is calm in my body.

Jackson, that one guy I sleep with———will physically push my toes to the ground to remind me how wound up I get. There is so much to accomplish and so many things to do that I cannot waste my time in a waiting room. At the pediatrician's office, I show up with five minutes to spare. That way the nasty, germy children can continue to share their diseases with others of their dirty little kind.

In the meantime, I'm simply waiting for the chiropractic office to open. My body is in its thirties, and I've been feeling sixty lately. My hips are out of whack. Yes, they take a pounding whenever Ella is at her dad's house. But I am not giving up sex, so something must be done. Oh, the wonders of medicine.

Now, my last chiropractic experience wasn't the best ever. I could barely sit in my car to drive home, and then I was curled up in bed, crying. The doc gave me some misplaced cortisone shots. Later it was discovered that he lost his license due to the unlawful sale of narcotics. Dude was selling prescription pain meds, yet he aggravated my pain.

APRIL 16, 2008

Yesterday I went to Stacey's house. Lasagna from my place and a salad from her fridge made a good meal. Stacey has severe ADHD. She was busy organizing her closets, again. Is there a better example of a homemaker task? Closet reorganization is unnecessary for everyday living. If it has been shoved to the back, you probably will not need it anytime soon. She had six bottles of the same after-bath spray scent. They go bad; they must have been on sale.

Stacey has valuable information to impart. The problem is that the listener can hear one of her stories twenty times and still not know the point of it. Yesterday, we began to get to the point of one of them. We used a tape recorder. She would talk, and then I would press pause and rewind. Maybe the information could be helpful with some of my own health concerns. I mean, what if I have a twisted fallopian tube? We always knew something in me was twisted.

Today Ella has a dentist appointment followed by Brownies, and then Mom picks her up, and Jackson will be here, and then her dad will come get her, take her to a hair appointment, and keep her for the night. I'm more excited than I should be about seeing my boyfriend. We never expected to have a warm, loving relationship with a partner. I'd always hoped for it but never expected anything remotely resembling this.

Being alone would have been better than being with my ex for the rest of my days. I'm sure that was the case—or would be, if I were ever alone. Unfortunately, I don't do well alone. Yup, this girl is one of those unfortunate people who must always be with someone. No time to heal, no time to reflect... just replace.

So, I go along from breakup to breakup, walking the trail from Mr. Reject to Mr. Right Now to "what have I done?" This shit ain't right. But what *is* right is my prescription for melancholy. Good sex often heals bad breakups. Now, you can't just go sleeping around. It's not safe, plus people talk—and we live in a small town.

To prevent this, you find a "he'll do for now." This prevents the whole sleep-with-a-couple-of-guys-feel-dirty-and-think-you-care-about-them-due-to-annoying-hormonal-fluctuations crap. Now you only have one or two issues.

No more feeling slutty, but now he knows your real name and where you live. That can also be a bad call, and let me tell you why.

Here are a few examples of the "he'll do for now" guy. Brad and Sam were both the "he'll do for now" heel. Sam is also referred to as Scammy. From my experience, the best way to get a man to commit is to make sure he knows you do not *want* to commit and you do not *need* to commit. If you can throw in a little gag reflex at the *M* word (marriage) and/or the *C* word (commitment), then that just seals the deal.

Seems like good, solid advice. But it backfires when you are not kidding and you really, *really* do not want to commit—especially not to *him*. Then you're embarrassed at the way he hangs around you, mimicking a sad puppy waiting for you to come back from somewhere else with someone else. Oh…and when he notices you've been out all night because you're in the same clothes and have a nappy spot at the back of your head, and he cries the kind of tears that puff up his face, and his nose drips—*be strong*.

More tips. Mr. Right Now should never have a key or know where you keep your hidden key. He should not be friends or make friends with any of your neighbors or your friends. He should not be related to your friends, your roommate, or yourself.

Convenience relationships can quickly become inconvenient. Brad was my roommate's cousin. When I was downstairs in my flat, he came to visit. When I was too busy to see him, he was upstairs visiting his other cousin. Bad Brad's jealousy was audible, because he stomped around in his big old work boots when I was prepping for dates. It's more difficult to knock boots with someone when you've got some man upstairs doing that with his own boots. I barely touched the kid, and he got to thinking we had something special.

Next up in our lineup is Sammy, a.k.a. Scammy. There are terrible stories about him, that even I am not ready to relate. My neighbors introduced him to me. I have still not forgiven them for that. When I booted him out of my bed at four in the morning—as is my right as the homeowner—he went directly to my neighbor's house to cry on her shoulder. Shit, it wasn't as if I could just get up and slink away after letting the wrong person into my bed. It was my house and my bed, and we all have to sober up some time.

Suddenly I am the bitch in these kinds of situations. Why? These whiny little children cannot accept that playtime is over. No—they have to go complain to everyone and look for sympathy. If we don't tell them our real names, they don't know where we live, and they cannot tell our people. It is as if it never happened.

Did you really think that I was going to tell a story about a relative? If I had one, he or she would have been sworn to secrecy. You are naughty. Naughty bits are not for bio relatives.

Lesson 10

THE HEART IS A MUSCLE; IT GROWS BACK

APRIL 17, 2008

I have some lovely dating tips, because my life is the perfect "what not to do" guide. My boy, Jax, is doing well, though, and I believe he's confident enough to let me work on this little project. He would prefer to think of me as virginal, but... he's willing to accept reality, especially when we have wild nights, like last night.

It seems Jack would appreciate my being a little more romantic. He brought up the fact that I often just snap my fingers and point to the bedroom. Who does that shit? Oh, yeah...me. Oh, God. He's got me pegged. Meanwhile, he lights candles, runs the bath, and paints my toes. And I just grab his package. He must feel so cheap. I love Jack, and I want him to feel loved, too. Having lived so long without romance, I find it's easy to forget what it was. He brought it up thoughtfully. It came out along the lines of, "Wow, that's cool. You never do that." That led into the deeper discussion.

In retrospect, I suppose I'm the girl with the boots, the pole, and the whip. Maybe I *am* a little aggressive. I'm just a little red Corvette, like the Prince song, and he wants to feel cherished.

I don't have a good source of income; therefore, it would be best for me to keep this one happy. Emergency, emergency! Plus, my birthday is next month, and "happy man buy happy gifts," and "nappy man buy nappy gifts."

APRIL 19, 2008

Dating can be fun when there's no pressure. My friend Jane had pressure. Jane wanted to be married. She went to college for her MRS. She even hired a service and treated her manhunt as a job hunt. See, I can't do that because of my unimpressive track record on both ends. She does have a decent guy and a cute little boy. Her plan worked.

The problem is that although men are sometimes retarded, they can still smell desperation. Even the dimmest of them notice they can get away with more shit. Jane met some decent guys, but they morphed into assholes. It's akin to exercise. We forget to exercise the sensitivity muscle. In other words, people do what they can get away with. Back to the doomed heroes Thelma and Louise: "You get what you settle for."

Adults are just large children, whether the male or female of the species. When married, I gained a child. Not a stepchild—no, my own spouse became a child, and at the tender age of twenty-four, this girl was nearly a child bride herself.

My spouse stopped resembling an adult. The bed was never made, the clothes were not put away, and I had to hide the candy. This was a man with a law degree from a prestigious university, for God's sake. When we met, he had a good job and decent friends. We laughed, danced, and talked for hours.

Sure, we had different backgrounds, but we had love. And love conquers all—until someone quits trying. He regressed. That's probably the best way to describe how many men seem to handle the transition to husband.

For example, he quit washing properly. The grooming was the first to go. Adult males should know how to clean behind and inside their own ears. There is a minimum length for all unwanted hair. If *unwanted hair* is a strange phrase to your personal adult male, then no one can blame you for wanting a piece of strange.

Regarding grooming of other body parts, if a girl can smell it from across the room, you can bet she won't be putting her face anywhere near it. And they wonder why we don't initiate more! Use the word *initiate* in a sentence. "My girl ate the burger initiate a bag of chips and a Twinkie." Improper grooming turns *initiate* into "Oh, no, she ain't!"

Thank God I won't make that mistake again. My man is the three-showers-a-day type. Now *I* feel dirty in comparison. That is how I roll—polar opposite on things. I was married to the world's most boring man. Now, I only date people with a past.

The job interview goes something like this: Do you have at least one parent in jail? Yes? You're in. Ever run a meth lab? Excellent! And how many kids? And the baby's mamma was a stripper? All the baby's mammas were strippers? Impressive!

When I started dating Jackson, he periodically sat me down and said, "I think you should know this." Then he would proceed to tell me a story. The hidden camera was never there. He was serious. The appropriate response was, "Thank you for sharing" and then "Why do you want me to know this?" The reason was always so that it would not get to me from someone else. The inappropriate response from me was, "Other people know this shit about you?"

Strangely, it's all accepted. He might cringe at my stories, but dude has mine beat by a landslide every time. Now that I'm no longer partnered to the world's most boring man, we have material for our own reality show.

Lesson 11

CLEAN YOUR OWN CLOSET, AND TAKE THE HIGH ROAD

APRIL 21, 2008

Good weekend. Crazy shit, though. My boyfriend dropped the *F* bomb. No, not the four-letter one. Those are common. He said *fiancée*. I had to take a big swig of water to wash the vomit out of my mouth—the kind you have to swish around to get the chunks back down. Because I'm a sensitive woman, I didn't roll down the window and spew. I swallowed the chunks. That must mean I love him. I swallowed.

Speaking of fellatio, I was once a Good Catholic Girl. My mother and grandmother have a strong faith in God. My mother often cringes when I speak, God love her. I am a Christian, just not of the Catholic variety. I prefer the garden variety, please. I'm in no position to preach, but when has that ever stopped anyone?

I have been married one time. We had irreconcilable differences. His job was to make money. My job was to do everything else. Homemaker—right. The glitch was that everything I did was examined and judged. Not a big deal if I'd had a trophy room and a stack of blue ribbons. Not so much. No matter how hard I worked, it was never enough.

The hardest lessons in life can come slowly. Oh, he didn't do that, either. However, to go after him about ED would be a cheap shot. I learned to be true to myself. I will never be a trophy wife or a blue-ribbon cow.

The man wanted a show horse but treated me like a workhorse. A pack mule, more like it. And it was not enough just to sit back in self-righteous judgment of another—he did not quietly sit back. No. He was all up in my face. "Are you sure you made enough for the whole family?" "Did you get all the RSVPs?" "Will every dish be hot at the same time?" "Do I have any clean, pressed shirts?" "How many carbs are in this?" Then, sometimes, I would get loving, helpful suggestions like, "It's missing something. What is it?" What did he want, three more courses, a pint of my blood, and another little piece of my soul?

It's easy to be a perfectionist when you never do a *goddamned thing*. Translation: please learn to accept yourself for who you are. Once you learn to do so, you will not be as hurt by lesser people's judgment of you. And if you truly achieve enlightenment, you will not have to think of them as lesser beings. I'm not there yet, just so you know. Self-acceptance will take a long time.

Haters are haters. Our consolation as nonhaters is that the haters hate themselves more than they hate you. They are miserable people who may just off themselves if we give them time. Catherine, the ex-monster-in-law, is a hater.

My ex has his old nickname: CARB, which stands for Cheap-Ass Rat Bastard. This name is especially fitting, because when his weight shoots through the roof, he always goes on a no-carb diet. I too am on a no-carb diet. No more cheap-ass rat bastards.

Now, we spent money. We just spent it all on meals out. I was packing on the pounds, too. Man, those home movies are scary. Picture Scarlett O'Hara saying passionately, "I'll never go hungry again." In our home, the motto was, "We'll never be hungry—ever."

Lately, CARB has earned a new nickname: Fake Jew. Three generations before my daughter was born, CARB had practicing Jews in his family. Judaism is an amazing religion. It is a deep, rich culture, and to be enriched in that way is a gift.

To pretend to be a Jew and pull it out on holidays and certain business transactions is a farce. To pretend to be a Jew and allow my child, born of a Christian mother, to believe she is one without providing any spiritual guidance is wrong. Silently, stealthily, I war with the Fake Jew. Okay, skip silently. If you have the impression that I do not do silent or stealthy well, you would be dead on.

Yesterday, five minutes before a birthday party, my princess informs me she will be forgoing leavened bread. She is eight, so it went more like, "Mommy, I can't eat anything they are serving, 'cuz I'm Jewish, and it's Passover."

My response was, "Well, I hope you're not hungry, because there will be yummy pizza and cake." What I wanted to say was, "There are no Jews in this house! Your mother was a shiksa! Your father is a sellout!" Kids eat pizza and cake. There's honoring your God and heritage, and then there's this bullshit.

Instead, I took the high road. No, I did not go out to my truck and light up a joint. I took the other high road. I thought about my next plan of attack. This plan includes a diagram, outline, and theoretical dissertation. The outline is on the fridge. The dissertation is on my computer. Both will be given to the Fake Jew this evening.

I have been bending over backward, except for last night at dinner. I made a completely new meal with no yeast, which I selflessly went shopping for and supplied. Anyway, at dinner, she explained Passover as the time God gave the Christians pimples and killed them because they were bad and mean to us Jews.

Some might call that an "aha" moment. To me, that was a WTF moment if I've ever heard one. Stunned, simply stunned. My face showed the horror. Ella burst into tears and began rubbing the wrinkles out of my forehead. I am going to kill her father! Cheap-Ass Rat Bastard Fake Jew! So, now she's being taught to hate the Christians because the bad, mean Christians gave the Jews pimples, and that's why she can't eat the foods she enjoys. Did I mention that she has no Jewish friends? All are run-of-the-mill Christians apart from one, whose family practices Jainism.

APRIL 22, 2008

The report was turned in to Mr. F. J. CARB yesterday. Stacey is going to love reading it. The recipient, however, took issue with being labeled a hypocrite. Okay, one more time, for good measure, the question must be asked: "How many times have they been to worship together?" None. Never. Nada. The point of my paperwork was not to vent. The point was to kick him on his spongy bottom.

Darrin called just before Jax showed up at my house. The bath was running, the candles were lit, and the wine was poured. Suddenly, fighting seemed useless. Make love, not war.

Bath, candles, wine...I must be some kind of romantic. I'm some kind of something. I'm trying a new thing by being proactive in the romance department. It's a wonderful feeling when your lover does all sorts of little things for you. It makes the grand gestures unnecessary.

Years of my life were spent not knowing just how pleasant it is to have someone consider you as they go about their business—for example, someone who drops off a bottle of shampoo in your shower because it's the kind you use and he can't wait to use it with you. The table being set, the dishes being done—those are the little things that spread joy.

Housework is an aphrodisiac when used as a spectator sport. Alternatively, it's awesome as a team sport. It makes you want to turn everything into a contact sport. Solo housework is a joy stealer. Sure, we girls cook, clean, and decorate to make the place look respectable, but that doesn't put the party in our pants. Seeing a man bent over the tub or sink and scrubbing...now, that is hot!

APRIL 23, 2008

This morning, I went through the closet to find things that are definitely not hot. Going through your old clothes does not put the party in your pants, either. It is unfun alone. Signing on to help your friends get rid of stuff is great, though. You can whoop and holler about the eighties stuff shoved in the back.

Stirrup pants—no.
Neon—no.
One-piece velour jumpsuit—no.
Cartoon character—no.
Picture of sexy lady in bikini on T-shirt with hole to fit your head—no.

See, this is easy. But it's hard to part with your old things, especially if you overpaid for them. Gay was easy when we did her closet. She was at or near her goal weight. When you're happy with your body, you can pull off nearly anything.

Spending time with Gay is, well gay. She's so neurotic; she makes me feel like the Dalai Lama. Doing Angelique's closet was more difficult. She, too, looks marvelous. She is in fantastic shape and just ran a three-mile race. Angelique is a man's man's dream. She looks fifteen years younger than her age. She is low maintenance. She is educated and does home improvement and landscaping as a hobby. No drinking or drug problems. No smoking.

In addition, she has no real shopping problems, either. Unless you include the fact that she does not shop. This is why cleaning her closet is difficult. She's simply too cute and petite for eighties shoulder pads. She was forgetting that it takes a few years for something to come back into style. We ended up making piles by asking a series of questions.

Does this fit?

Where do I plan to wear it?

Will my friends be embarrassed to be seen with me when I wear it?

What does this go with?

When Angelique asked the question about her neon RELAX shirt, my answer was, "A match." We need to burn the evidence, quickly.

APRIL 24, 2008

Money is a big factor in anyone's life. Well…maybe not *any*one's. It never used to matter much in mine. Now it does. I miss the landscapers working in my yard, blowing leaves and making everything pretty. I miss my housekeeper, my exotic vacations, the Aveda Spa, the Somerset Collection, linen tablecloths and napkins, and crystal. Sometimes our life becomes something we were not expecting

APRIL 28, 2008

Monday morning. The day starts with a lot of snuggling with my boyfriend. My head on his chest, pressed up behind him, him spooning me—that's a delicious way to start the morning.

Not long after, my ex calls to report that our daughter has a stomachache and he needs a second opinion. She was up before six complaining of an icky feeling. Jackson had left, so I said, "Bring her on over, and I'll handle everything." After some mommy-daughter time, she was dancing in the dining room to her iPod. Busted—she was in school before the first bell.

Last night, Jackson and I went for a walk. We chatted with neighbors as we strolled along. We had a beer and hung out with Brad (Stacey's husband) and his folks and Jennie (their daughter). During this time, we made plans to help with the proposed garage sale...the one that's always spoken of but never occurs.

My part in the plan is to bring Stacey to Lily's house. Lily is her great-aunt, who owns a home on the other side of town. She lives in a "home" but still has her own. There, we will meet Candace, Stacey's mom-in-law, and her mom, Jill. Jill has a key to the house. The rest of the people are slated to be there around ten thirty. My plan was to be there by nine. At nine thirty, I spoke to Stacey for a second time that morning, the first having been an hour earlier. She hadn't yet left her house for her second errand of the day. The first order of business had been to get the kid to school. Since she was still at home after I'd dropped mine off, we knew the schedule was already off. Now, she's showered, but the rest of the getting ready hasn't happened yet.

That means by the time she's anywhere near ready to leave the house again, it will be lunchtime. This may help explain why I say projects that are spoken about but never actually happen. I'm skipping the makeup because we're going to an old, dusty house. Besides, no one needs to waste makeup on a workhorse day. Yesterday was my cute day. That should last me for the week.

Lesson 12

RULES NEED NOT BE FOLLOWED
BUT MUST BE KNOWN

APRIL 29, 2008

Penny and Stacey were over for dinner last night. I met Penny through ADHD Stacey. They have been friends for years and met through the line dance network. We made pizza, breadsticks, and salad. The kids had corn on the cob as an appetizer. Penny noticed they're easier to deal with before we feed them. The semicomatose state my child goes into without food is scary. Her body metabolizes food in seconds. Before she loses all her energy, she gets super whiny. Drama, drama, drama. We have lots of healthy snacks on tap to prevent meltdowns. As long as nutrients are ingested, her little world spins properly.

The kid isn't being singled out. Her mom and grandma have the same issue. We both get snippy first. My child runs into a corner and cries; others such as myself make other people want to run and hide.

MAY 2, 2008

Today I am not working, not dropping a second grader off, and not picking her up after school. Looks like a cake day to me. Of course, I won't let it be easy. I want to be doing *something*. Life is too short to watch television.

So, I may go to the job-search center, sand my floors, go to the gynecologist, and recaulk my tub. This will turn my lovely day into a proper shit cake.

Gay called last night. She cannot comprehend my wanting to work. She misses the time we used to spend shopping and planning children's parties. It's not just the money. When you do something you love and you're stretching your mind, it's rewarding. At least, that's what I hear. God knows I've never done it. But I still believe. Compare it to a happy marriage. I've never done it, but I believe wholeheartedly that it is possible.

A bunch of people called last night. Jackson was here after work. We hung out while Ella played with the neighbor boy Mick. We stacked wood, and I baked bread. Earlier, Ella and I had worked on her homework.

Lainie called with good news and gossip. She has always been my most responsible friend, even back in school. She owns her own home, has paid off her truck, has survived both cancer and divorce, has a good relationship with her family, and has an impressive job at a credit union. Last time we got together, I volunteered to babysit her while she proceeded to get wasted, hit on her frenemy's little brother, and almost puked in a public restroom.

Lainie's frenemy has moved up to enemy status. She started with, "I'm angry with you because you didn't share intimate details with me regarding your sex life." So, the frenemy feels betrayed. She heard Lainie's gossip through someone else. It all makes sense.

Add to this the fact that Jess, the frenemy, has slept with the same man in a friends-with-benefits fashion. In addition, Jess was the one who introduced them. So, we have a girl who is mad because you're not sharing secrets. Friends are supposed to share secrets.

However, that secret may make her angry. Sleeping with her booty boy on a regular basis aces her out of her FWB (friends-with-benefits) booty-call deal. Oh...and they work together. Not the booty-call man but the people who are sharing this gossip. Since he does not work at the bank, and people know Lainie is getting some action, Jess has decided to fight back by telling everyone that Lainie is sleeping with a five-hundred-pound black dude.

Yes, they work at a financial institution, and the trainer, Jess, is telling exaggerated details regarding a manager's sex life. She wasn't lying; she just added a few extra pounds on the person for good measure and chose the color to prey on people's bigotry.

Before Lainie hit on Jess's twenty-two-year-old brother at the bar, Jess seemed content to focus on the "Lainie does not exist" theory—you know, the one where you speak to everyone except the victim. Jess took it to a completely new level with introductions. And having a periphery member of the group was perfect. That was my job.

It went like this: "You remember Jewel; I told you all about her. We went on the drunken hayride…" Then she completely bypassed Lainie, the one who'd brought me to the hayride. Now, to (almost) everyone's credit, they spoke to Lainie as if she were a nonleper. But Jess was *not* going to lose another sex partner to Lainie and forbade her current partner to speak with Lainie.

Lainie flirts. Let me repeat. She *flirts*. It's a part of her nature. When you add alcohol, she flirts and becomes a hanger. She will drape herself on men. We've discussed it. She is aware.

My ex-friend Ann was a hanger, except no alcohol was needed to make her project as an InstaWhore. She was a natural-born whore. I can't even tell you when it started, but we were just young teens when she was picking up men at the roller rink. Picture a girl so scarecrow skinny that you didn't even know she was there…until the skeletal arms come across your man's chest. Then you knew. To each his or her own, I say…until you touch something *I* own. At fourteen, I went on a class trip to Europe, and while I was in Paris, she and my boyfriend got bare-assed. We didn't hang out much after that.

When the class returned from the trip, my boyfriend was ready to take the next step in our relationship. Translation: he wanted to start doing with me what he was doing with my friends. He had it planned out. When I nixed the idea (hellooo…fourteen?), he dropped me off and took a ride with another "friend" of mine. We all had frenemies even before the term was coined. The boyfriend and Katie ended up in her hot tub that afternoon. We all know Katie was active because she was also sleeping with my brother.

Ew. I had to hear the details because my friend was sleeping with my brother's best friend. These four double-dated, double-dog-dated, or whatever. In retrospect, I have no idea where I got my self-respect.

A good 75 percent of my girlfriends were excessively active sexually. What is excessive? In high school, some of the limits could be the following:

* No sex until marriage
* No sex until adulthood
* No sex without a condom
* No sex with married men
* No sex with someone else's beau (a.k.a. OPP)
* No sex with more than one partner

Anyone see a pattern here? You pass the test if you can remember the NO SEX part. I was a couple months shy of graduation when I first had sex, and that was still too soon. Life is confusing enough for young adults. Sex does not make life easier.

If my first was the worst, then my last is a blast. My first adult boyfriend was a bad call all around. See, this is a good example of why girls should not date in high school.

Jackson's daughter, Amy, is fourteen. She is cute, athletic, smart, and respectful. Her friends come off the same way. We are so glad she has no interest in dating. That won't last long, but it's good right now.

I hope that Miss Amy will have better boundaries than her parents did. Each of her parents had unplanned-pregnancy issues. Dad was tossed into the hoosegow once for nonsupport. Then test results showed he was not the baby's daddy. Yet another indication that my rules for high school are valid—and can be used later in life as well.

Last night, my prince told me, "Sometimes you are just too much. What am I going to do with you?" My suggestion was that long term, he had only two options: adopt me or marry me.

Since he hadn't followed my rules in high school—or later—age-wise I could be his daughter, so the adoption thing could work. Notice the word *legitimately* was not used. Who is better at being a dependent than someone who has no *job*? I could get death benefits and all that veteran stuff. God knows, this girl threw in a "please, Daddy, please?" Was that too much? Maybe he shouldn't say

I'm too much. He's not sold on the adoption thing, as that would make him a grandpa, and the incest thing is not a turn-on.

MAY 5, 2008

Cinco de Mayo. Tonight it was celebrated with Mexican beer, chicken enchiladas, chicken-and-cheese tacos, and salad. Stacey and Jennie came over to eat with us. The laundry was beginning to take over my girlfriend's home, so I offered to take her child so that she could focus. She got three loads done. Not bad. The clothes are not put away, but they're clean.

Just call me Super Nanny with all the kids at my house. They are good. However, I do have to get after them about leaving messes and not closing doors. Heads are gonna roll if one little boy doesn't start shutting every door he opens. So, today was not much of a party for this mom. But Saturday at Hester's was. We'll just take comfort in that.

Later, Jax came over. He did four overnights in a row. Ella was here only half the time. Ella is still undecided regarding my boyfriend. Jack does help her with things, and her mom is always laughing. She finds something else to do when we start spontaneously slow dancing on the deck. The only bad thing might be that she filled two shot glosses with Crystal Light and said, "Bottoms up!" to me last night. *Mom of the year!*

For the record, she also calls medicine cups shot glasses, and she's taking amoxicillin for her strep. So, I'm really not as bad as I make myself out to be. Usually I hide my drinking like everyone else's mom.

Darrin volunteered to take her overnight so that I could attend my annual Cinco de Mayo party. Wow. Seems so un-Darrin-like. I took him up on it. He dropped her off the next morning and brought a huge thing of meatloaf for us. With all these yummy leftovers, I have not had to cook. Much of Sunday was spent doing crafts with Ella while Jackson recovered from the party in bed. Then he and I rescreened a door while Ella played with friends outside.

Lesson 13

NEVER BE AFRAID TO GET A
NEW RIDE OR SIDE HUSTLE

MAY 8, 2008

It's time for a new car. For what I spend in a year on maintaining my car, I can outright buy a new one. She will be a little shit box with wheels but such a deal. My current lease, registration, plates, and insurance cost over five grand a year. Add that to spending seventy bucks at the gas pump to fill the tank each time. Yup, I am the proud owner of an SUV. Lease payments are currently quite low. That means you're spending more on your tank of gas than your monthly payment—maybe five times more.

Homes are foreclosing, jobs are disappearing, gas is pricey, and grocery prices have shot through the roof. What a fantastic time to be a single, unemployed mom with three times the necessary house and three times the necessary car!

MAY 12, 2008

It was good to see most of the girls, even for only a little while. Ward loved the scrapbook I made him and enjoyed his fiftieth birthday party. The smart couple (Ward and Eve, not Jackson and Jewel) took Monday off too, thinking an extra day to recover might be in order. I was just there this morning to pick up the set of keys I'd left. Well, at least it wasn't my whole purse, and at least I didn't drive home. Ward loved his coffin cooler so much he asked if he could keep it. The scrapbook was a huge hit, and everyone got a chance to look at it. The party went on until six in the morning. I didn't make it that far—I was carried out just after midnight. *Nice!*

I faked feeling chipper on Mother's Day. It seemed wrong to say, "Go entertain yourself—Mommy has a hangover." So, I sucked it up and played with Ella all afternoon and evening. This morning, she said, "Can you believe some mommies would want the day off *away* from their kids?" She kept saying she'd had the best day ever. What a good kid!

She said, "Mommy, you should sit down and not work at all, but I do kinda want (fill in the blank)."

I said, "What happened to the no-work thing?"

She batted her eyes and said, "Jackson?" She's a funny girl.

He got up and got what she wanted.

Then he showed us a couple of cool things in the *MetroParent* "Things to Do" guide. We decided it might be fun to go to a dude ranch or drive-in movie. She got excited about all of us going together.

Jax got what he wanted.

Said child has been standoffish with said boyfriend. She's slowly warming.

This is the guy who taught her how to ride a bike and who does her math homework with her. She has only recently begun to say, "Thank you, Jackson."

Jax made himself scarce by working in the garage and kitchen and then left to give us some girl time. I'm liking this boy. He took care of me when I overindulged (like a moron). With reinforcements, he packed up my stuff and got me out to the car. He sped me home and rubbed my back as I proceeded to hurl out his window. The next morning, I got breakfast in bed, and the coffee was lifted to my lips for me. When Darrin dropped Ella off, he went to the garage to fix my mower, and I opened the gifts from her that she and Daddy had picked out. She gave me some cool stuff from Bath & Body Works, a board game, and framed prose. A card and a hug would have been fine. But this was sweet.

I needed to clarify that Mr. Cohen was not the "he" that fixed the mower. Darrin has no mechanical ability. Jackson allowed the ex and the child to give me my gifts together while he went to go fix stuff. Jax still asks, "Why did he ever let you go?" Darrin no longer had a choice. When this girl is done, she is done.

My latest car research has focused on the Chevy Aveo. The gas mileage is phenomenal, and it's cheap as hell. I could purchase it for less than I spent on lease payments, registration, and insurance last year. Moreover, I put money down on my last lease! This little (and I do mean little) baby has a good warranty, and I could use my incentives as a current GM customer.

On Tuesday, I'll help out at the school and then go take a test drive. It seems I was hosed on the stimulus check when the US government only gave me $600. For a parent, that should have been $900, by my calculations. Something about my not making enough money. Dude, that's why I need the funds! The only Bush I trust is my own, certainly neither of the Georges.

MAY 16, 2008

This morning, my calls were to Stacey to see how much coffee to make in case she was visiting and to the moms in the Brownie troop. For the last couple of years, no one has done anything thoughtful for the troop leader as a thank you. That is unacceptable. This year, I took on the job of rallying the troops to get a gift. Yes, I am also volunteering at the school and helping Stacey with her great-aunt and her house stuff. Since I have not found a real job, I'm considering childcare for two extra kids. I've done this before and enjoyed it. Kids are terrific.

The money would be better than nothing, and I'd get to spend time with my own child. Win-win. In the meantime, my boyfriend called to tell me to use the credit card he gave me to buy dinner and drinks this evening.

A get-together for employees of ExpressTech is happening. Okay…well, mostly ex-ExpressTech employees. I worked there in 1996. That was the same year I got married. A lot was going on that year. The best thing about 1996 was meeting McKenna. She is a book in and of herself, but I'd never dare analyze or interpret her actions, partly because that would get my sorry ass kicked. She is who she is, and I love and respect her for that.

Anyway, weren't we talking about me? My résumé looks good. My real career history is a bit spottier. Let me try to recreate it. We'll dissect my life in order to kick my own ass:

* Got paid to iron (ten cents per shirt)
* Babysat once for a newborn
* Received a spotty allowance for dusting and stuff
* Was assistant to a sales representative for chemical equipment
* Clerked in an ice-cream store
* Was a full-time summer nanny
* Then did lots more clerking (retail sales, acting, recruiting, accounting, public relations, reception, data entry)

One retail establishment let me go when I asked to sneak in the back and grab a bite of apple. I weighed one bill and was feeling woozy. They didn't believe in breaks. At one recruitment firm, my interviews were too in depth. Any interview over three minutes was excessive, and I am a talker.

I was purchased via a headhunting fee to work at a worker compensation consulting service. After acquiring certain knowledge (i.e., that I was not a floozy), the owner let me go. He had a history of sleeping with employees—so much so that his wife started working at the company to keep an eye on him. Our job was to get injured workers back to work. Mostly, we busted fakers.

All the people we interviewed seemed uninterested in getting back to work. Many had been grossly overpaid for what they'd done originally and were hoping for an early, easy retirement. C'mon, so you lost a leg or a finger. Move on. Get over it. My client is done paying for you to sit on your ass and drink your troubles away. Yup, spoken from the same girl whose best friend is Brother Jack, as in Jack Daniel's. Never said I was not a hypocrite. "Hey pot. It's the kettle calling. You black!"

The next consulting firm I worked for did not exactly fire people. They were happy to keep them on. They just weren't going to pay them anymore. They said, "No more salaries, and here is your new commission schedule."

Because my pay was hourly and not commission based, they tried to push me out.

Now, this girl has lived with the biggest asshole on the planet. I can take the pressure. So, I did my best and ignored the insults until they gave up and let me go. This way I could collect unemployment and an extra two weeks' pay. Someone put in the handbook that we all got severance if we were let go. It pays to read the handbook.

My attorney had to work with theirs to get it, though. But at stake was over a $1,000, so it was well worth the effort. Now, this same attorney needs his kids chaperoned this summer. I've got the other previous employer who owes me over three thousand. You'd better bet we're adding his services into the package deal.

An attorney can run a creditor exam to try to get three grand. I could try using Big G., Darrin's attorney, and Big G can be vicious. He has always been sweet and kind to me, but I wouldn't dare cross him. People are lined up to beat the crap out of my ex-boss, the prince of Internet porn. But I just want my money. Now, if they accidentally ran into him with a big truck...

So far, I have garnished his bank account and come up with a grand total of $16.63. It cost me $15.00 to put in the paperwork.

First, I was careful not to burn any bridges, but now I would burn his fucking house down if they hadn't already foreclosed on it. Thank goodness I am not bitter. He's safe only because I am lighter impaired. Easy push-button lighters are my friend. The other ones might hurt me because they put fire too close to my fingers. This has kept me from becoming a smoker. No smoking, and no arson. That will have to go on my profile if I ever join a dating site. Of course, if we're still having this much fun, Jackson and I might want to...ugh, excuse me...there's some bile in my throat...

Lesson 14

LIFE IS MORE SOUFFLÉ THAN MICROWAVE MEAL, OR KARMA HAS NO HOTLINE

MAY 20, 2008

Today I turned thirty-six years old. Ella baked a cake and made meatloaf (with my help). Darrin wished me happy b-day before Jack did. Because guys are sometimes slow and usually put stuff off, he called to say he was leaving work early to buy my gift. 'Cuz, of course, he didn't have a whole year's notice. I told him to just get here and not worry about it.

My child was making me a card on the computer and wanted some help. As I could not help her without seeing the surprise, and I am the closest thing to an adult in my home, we had her call Darrin. He was—big shock—useless. I was watching my friend's child, so I asked her father to assist Ella. Big mistake. She wanted help with fonts and spacing. He told her she was too old to call me mommy and proceeded to delete her work. Whoa. That was unnecessary. I whispered in her ear, "Baby girl, go get into Mommy's bed, and she will deal with this." He tried to apologize but managed to make it worse. His wife dealt with him later.

Ella will always be my baby. I don't care if she's riding a bike, driving a car, or watching porn. She's my baby, and I enjoy being Mommy.

MAY 27, 2008

What a week. It was a long weekend, too. Last week, I felt much loved with all my well-wishers. The phone was ringing off the hook. Yay me!

Tuesday, the twentieth, was a little hectic. I went to Stacey's to help with the home office they are building. After dropping Ella off at school, I went to Stacey's place as scheduled. She decided not to return home after school, instead staying and chatting with other moms in the classroom. This is a special game for some bored homemakers: disturbing the teachers as they are preparing the classroom for the next day. So, I waited in her driveway and called repeatedly.

When she finally came home, she cleaned out the sink and did other little things to avoid the office. Procrastination is alive and well. I get it. I do it, too. Then she talked on the phone for hours discussing how busy she was. Meanwhile, the project was getting no closer to completion. After the sixth phone call to and from Lord knows whom, bitching about how she was *so* busy, I slipped her a note and left.

People can become very adept at doing nothing. When you're a member of a family, you are part of a team. And when you choose not to participate, you are letting the team down.

This stuff hits home for me because my own marital teammate stopped participating, and picking up all the slack was hard. It made me angry to watch him sleep, sit, stare, read, and breathe. Especially the breathing—that pissed me off the most.

When my friend Stacey's spouse, in-laws, and mutual friends ask what she does all day, I just shake my head. Now, when she's at my place, she's a godsend. She dusts, sweeps, picks up, clips coupons, power shops, and party plans. She spackles, she paints, she cooks, she scrapbooks. The girl can go, go, go. Her potential is amazing. *She* is amazing.

Yet her inability to get anywhere or do anything on time drives me *insane*. I have a commitment phobia, and she makes me look clingy. For example, it took her seven years to accept her husband's marriage proposal. He stuck it out. That was impressive. He also stuck it in and got her pregnant. That helped to force the marriage issue a little.

Yesterday, Jax and I discussed the snip-snip. He was the one who brought it up. I am all for it, and he knows that. He is done. No more babies in this relationship. Ever the romantic, I said, "You've been known to drink and drive. You die, and I have to start over. Let's keep my parts intact." He suggested a shot to make my periods go away. Nah, this IUD thing seems to work, and it's got a few more good years on it. After forty, I'll look at other options.

On Thursday, I went on a field trip with the second graders. It's been a while since I've been on the bus. The kids are well behaved. All they want at this age is attention—from the teacher, from a parent, from each other. The best gift anyone can give is time. I am so fortunate to have time to spend with my daughter and her friends.

The summer has only just begun, and we cook, read, play, swim, and snuggle. This week we had a lot of mommy-daughter time. It felt good. Daddy was on a cross-country trip. He got back yesterday and called to set up a day to see her. Tonight is perfect. This way I get time to spend alone with my man, and tomorrow I can go to a placement agency.

On Friday, Ella and I used my gift certificate to Great Lakes Crossing Mall. We did lunch and bought cool stuff. In the morning, we picked up Momma's new car. We are the proud owners of a bright-red Chevy Cobalt. My cousin showed her how to get out of the trunk if her mom ever locks her in.

We spent Saturday at the fair and were back in time for Jax to see the hockey game. He came back here after the game and took Ella out for breakfast while Mommy met a group of friends for breakfast at the Clarkston Union. I was back from breakfast in time to get him back to his place for a pool party for his daughter, Amy.

Ella and I met Jax at his place after I painted parts of my ceiling. Then I helped with the party a little, and the kids ate and swam. After the party died down, I played with Ella in the pool. That was our favorite part. Then we all watched *High School Musical*, and Amy left for her mom's house. Ella and I slept over.

The next day, we woke up to a breakfast of Dunkin' Donuts and prepared for the next party. Ella and I got ready, and we bolted back home. Jax showered at his pace and caught up with us as I finished packing the car. We had just one stop to make, and then we were off. Our timing was dead on. We got back in time for a tiny rest before Jax went to meet with his friends to see the next hockey game. The Wings are in the playoffs, and he wants to share the excitement with someone who gives a shit. That would exclude his girlfriend, because she couldn't care less.

Lesson 15

CELEBRATE THE WINS

MAY 30, 2008

Tomorrow we're throwing a bonfire. There should be about fifteen people coming, and anyone can spend the night. Most of my major home improvements are done. That means today is the day to put back my ladder, move the rest of the furniture, and put away the painting supplies.

Normal people would just sweep and buy beer, right? I wonder what it's like for them. Each improvement project leads to another in my world. Last night, for example…

Last night I dropped a wrench from the light fixture in the foyer down onto the hardwood steps. Yes, it made a mark. Just lovely. The last time the house was partially painted, the painters' tape was left on too long, and removing it ripped paint off the ceiling. That led to spackling, sanding, and painting the ceiling in those rooms. Why can't I just sit and watch *Good Morning America* like other suburban ladies?

I was accused of having "that look in my eye." When my man friend mimicked my look, even *I* was frightened. Seems I was accidentally projecting the "I'm going to kill you now" look. He has only seen that look one other time, and it was directed at him. Maybe he'll lend me the genteel letter I wrote to him to describe my feelings…or maybe I'll just take it back after I kill him.

JUNE 3, 2008

This morning, Grapenuts are crunching under my feet. Earlier, my child felt something sharp on her feet, and it turned out to be hardened rice from left-over Chinese food. These are all indications that the house could use a good once-over.

It was almost sparkling on Saturday afternoon, when I had twenty or so friends over for a bonfire and to watch the Wings game. We are still winning... well, depending on what happened last night after I went to sleep. I should check to see if there was partying in the streets of Detroit. All we need is another riot.

Overall, Saturday night was a grand success. It was the first time Jackson and I mixed our friends. It was time. His friends enjoyed mine because *my friends rock!* My biggest blessing in life has been the ability to get to know good people with good hearts. Some of my cousins were here who have known me all their lives—and they still come by.

Lainie and Mac have known me since my early twenties. Lainie and Mac are the jock types. Trust me—they are *all woman.* By that I mean that Mac is high maintenance on the hair, nails, and jewelry thing. Her body is killer and just screams, "I am woman!" Lainie is a sex fiend. She loves men. She flirts with men. She is *randy*!

How nice that I am such a labeler. Speaking of labels...yesterday I watched *Sex and the City*, the movie, with Stacey. Loved it! When dating, I used *Sex and the City* terms to describe myself. When I went out with my friend's brother, I told him, "I'm a cross between Charlotte and Samantha." That seems to be a safe yet interesting description.

My girls would see me as Carrie because I write. However, I cannot afford Carrie's lifestyle and do not wear the crazy shit that comes out of her closet. Ten grand on an outfit, and we have seen carnies that look better dressed. Wow. Also, I don't have the man-face thing going on. For the record, the actress herself is amazing. Sarah Jessica Parker has done it all. And by *all*, that includes *Square Pegs* when she was a teen.

Miranda's negativity regarding men is something I can relate to. Plus, she was the first one to have a kid. That would be a similarity. I am a happy, bouncy positive until it comes to my own relationships with men.

Charlotte is a Pollyanna and sees the good in everyone. That would be me. Also, I have the little innocent look down. This girl is the blond Snow White. Here I am, singing out the window, calling the woodland creatures. This look and persona make me a wonderful addition to class trips and Brownie outings. Jackson's family and friends say, "She is just the sweetest thing," and I am—mostly. The ugly is well hidden.

But it's easier to be Samantha with people who know me well. The bawdy jokes, gory details, close friendships with adult toy store clerks...yup, I have led couples through the video store's back room to help them make a good porn pick. But no, we did not watch it together. Certain lines need to be drawn...I think.

At the bonfire, I was energetic and efficient at first. Then I slowed down and relaxed. When I sat down, I got myself a lap dance from Penny. So, I got up—after I ran out of singles. Well, duh.

Sure, then I get my ass squeezed by my cousin. So, I go sit my butt back down and get it put on Ward's lap next to Stacey. That's about the time Ward winks at Eve and says, "Baby, you're gonna get some tonight," and she deadpans, "Stop threatening me."

Once again, these are my people. I made it to bed around four in the morning and gave up on whoever was still going strong. I was not awake enough to translate the slurring into coherent language. Dirk thought I was going to get busy with my man, but I showed him my snoring, sprawled-out partner, and we knew neither of us was going to get any action. I was wrong...did I mention that another randy friend was there? Jackson made up for it many times over in a matter of hours. At breakfast, I stated, "God, I'm whipped. The only thing I'm good for is light porn." Sunday morning porn has become a tradition. Doesn't everyone get on their knees on Sunday morning? Don't most call out the Lord's name in praise?

JUNE 11, 2008

How did I live through the weekend? On Friday, I got a call at seven thirty in the morning asking if I wanted to go to the Stanley Cup parade. "Yes," I said. "When are we leaving?" Stacey says, "Why don't you guys meet Jennie and me..." *Screech, boom, bam.* School is not out yet. It's Friday. What kind of crazy, irresponsible mother takes her kid out of school to watch a parade in ninety-six-degree weather? So, here I am in the minivan with Stacey, Jennie, and Ella...

Yes, I'm one of those crazies. In retrospect, it was really not the best call. However, Ella didn't miss much at school, and she wasn't the only child out that day. But the kiddies were roasting and couldn't see the parade very well.

Stacey made them little shelters out of my blanket and boxes. They were in downtown Detroit outside Comerica Park in their little homeless-person shack. Add some snackies, and you are golden. Plus, the shelter was right by the ice-cream truck.

Stacey spent the whole time placating the whiny children while I watched the parade. I was tired of the whiny children and refused to cater to them. Did I mention that I don't know or care about the game or the players? Luckily there are plenty of people happy to teach me.

After the parade was over, I got the kids in line for icy treats. Jennie had a hissy fit, and the day went downhill from there. Something about wanting a nutty bar even if her air passages closed up and she died on the street, at which point her mother was finally done placating her and said, "You will get *nothing*, you ungrateful wretch!" and pulls them out of the exceedingly long line that I had taken care to get them at the front of before the throngs closed in.

As the mom and daughter bickered, I put my kid back into the line, because she was not an ungrateful wretch and should not have to pay for Jennie's attitude. Plus, experience with other moms has shown me that 95 percent of the time, punishment is only threatened and rarely followed through on. When parents do that, we are just wasting time and proving that what we say can be taken lightly. As we were exiting the city, her child broke free and ran away again. Not an ideal place to lose your child.

DOGGEDLY TRY TO STAY SANE (OR FAKE IT)

JUNE 14, 2008

I asked my friends what they wanted for the summer. Mac wants to hear Angelique tell stories and eat chocolate. Angelique wants to save money and learn to relax. Ryan, her boyfriend, wants to play golf. McKenna said that in this life, some people are very good at putting themselves in other people's shoes. Then there's my friend Angelique, who steals shoes. Her dog, Bennie, chews shoes. And Sarafina, Fancy Fina, buys shoes.

JUNE 18, 2008

Late Sunday afternoon or early evening. Mac and I returned from visiting Angelique. No one in their right mind could hate Angelique. She is a mothering sort. She takes care of people, like her mother, both brothers, and her nephew. She is a devoted parent to her dog, Bennie. She and her boyfriend love her dog so much that I penned a poem for him in their honor.

A Father's Day Poem from the Bennie Boy

You treat me like a baby,
You let me kiss your face,

You keep my momma happy,
She sits upon your face.

You sometimes let me be the first
Because I'm Momma's little man;
You'd think we had a ménage à trois
With a jar of Peter Pan.

You make my momma cum while sprawled,
You rarely scream when you take a shit,
You built me an agility jump and tunnel;
Every day you take a hit.

Dad, I hope you always stick with us;
We'll always be a team.
You let me chase chippies, SQs, and coons—
At least coons keep themselves clean

Love,
Bennie

Not at all classy. Angelique revised it to make it a little more meaningful. Her version is much sweeter.

A Father's Day Poem from the Bennie Boy

You treat me like you've known me
My entire life,
And from what I hear,
You want Mom to be your wife.

At first you were afraid
To be entrusted with my care,

But now we see the real truth—
We make up quite a pair!

The things you do, the love you show,
The people food that makes my belly grow,
All goes to prove you're a special guy;
I can see it in my mama's eye.

Dad, I hope you'll always stick with us;
We'll always be a team.
I have to say my life is good—
It's better than a dream!

I love you, Daddy!

Mac asked me how I honestly feel about OPP (other people's pets).

"Do you really want to know?" I asked.

"We've got time," he answered. We had the whole ride back from Cleveland to Detroit.

Animals are wonderful. It's their people that kill me! Every dog has six legs—their own four and their owner's two legs to support them. Just yesterday, I scooped up the poop in my yard (did I mention that I don't own a dog?) and put it on my neighbor's porch. That felt good, so I also cleaned up the poop in another neighbor's yard and put that poop on her front step. Then I went hunting for another pile to pop into her birdbath. It was liberating.

Everyone poops. When you let your pet out to poop and you don't find it in your yard, the poop went somewhere else. There is no magical poop fairy. So... pick it up! I get a warm feeling in my heart when I see responsible pet owners carrying plastic bags. Anything less is wrong. If this hint is not enough for my neighbor, I have numerous friends with large dogs, and I will block her doors and garage with shit.

Animals are lovely, but they are not humans. People who cannot parent sometimes own pets. Sound bitchy? Maybe so. But check out these examples, and see if you can throw in a few of your own.

One friend has numerous cats and no kids. She loves those kitties to no end. But she kicks them when they hike their legs up to clean themselves "because it looks wrong," she says. Since when is cleaning yourself wrong?

Another friend has three cats and has spent a mint on special surgeries. In addition, she divided her home up using special gates and doorways to ensure they each have privacy. There is a schedule delineating who gets to sleep with the mommy when. Cat people are often single people who started out seemingly normal.

Dog people are a whole other breed. In the lunchroom at work, when they overhear a story about real live people, they interject with a story about their dogs. It sounds something like this:

"Stacey, do you have a new granddaughter? I remember when we first brought home Knuckles, my mom's first granddogger. That Knuckles was up all night, whining."

It's a fucking dog! A *dog*! Not a human child! When in doubt, ask yourself these questions:

* Did you give birth to it?
* Are you sacrificing for it?
* Will you be putting braces on it?
* Must you explain good and evil to it?
* Will you ensure it does not breed inappropriately?
* Will you be teaching it to tie its shoes and ride a bike?
* Will you take it to church, temple, or mosque?
* Do you take it to a pediatrician?
* Do you check out the school system before moving?
* Do you make sure it doesn't go potty on other people's property?

Being a natural birth parent of a nondisabled child in a suburban neighborhood, I can answer yes to all these questions. Good pet owners are expected to have one or two yeses, maybe even three. Decent parents are expected to have more yeses than their dog-owner counterparts. If you're a good dog owner *and* a good parent, your ticket to heaven is paid in full.

People say, "Love me; love my pet." No. Not so much. Crotch sniffers are the worst. In my presence, they get their heads gently turned away until only a punch or knee to the muzzle works. Once the dog's jaw cracks up in the air, they stop the shenanigans.

People create these problems. Dogs do not. Properly trained animals are lovely. Dogs who beg have been fed scraps. Dogs that crotch sniff have probably been allowed to do more by their lonely owners. Look for extra-big jars of peanut butter or honey in the pantry. If you see them, consider wearing a cup.

In Egypt, cats were worshipped. Cat worshippers are quiet people. They sit home and play with their brood of kitties, and that is their option—if they are okay with a house that smells of cat. But there are worse things. At least with cats, you don't have to buy peanut butter. They appreciate the smell of tuna.

Dogs could be bred for eating, the way cows are in America. Otherwise, people do some weird shit. Like Angelique, who worships her dog. He is smart, that I will grant her. Bennie is smarter than her brothers or many of her (okay, our) ex-boyfriends. But he is still a dog.

I refuse to feed Bennie, because they have some elaborate seven-step regimen that must occur before ingestion. That is stupid, and I'll have no part of it. Being thrilled at the speed at which he can needlessly hunt and kill innocent creatures is a little freaky, too.

Bennie has scrapbooks made in his honor, and Angelique has family photos taken with just herself and her dog. The Christmas pictures are kinda cute the first time around. The yearly ones, though? What are we to say? "My, look how much he's grown"? No, because he is a *dog*!

This is not a tirade against Angelique, as she is a doll. We'll choose a new victim: Lainie. Lainie is also a fantastic human being, but her dog, Champ, is a nasty little mutt. Mutt owners are to be applauded. *Any* pet rescuer is to be applauded. Rescuing a dog is a hundred times better than supporting puppy mills. Same goes for cats. What kind of selfish do you have to be to promote overbreeding in horrid conditions like that? I suppose they eat meat too, and a lot of it. That's it, we're calling PETA! But I digress…

Anyway, Lainie has this mutt, Champ. She and her ex-husband argued about it in the divorce proceedings. She would spend hours and days worrying about whether she would lose her beloved dog. That was wasted time they can never get back

My divorce included custody of a human being. Vastly different...people. Her ex got an apartment. They do not accept dogs—as dogs are not people. Being a loving person, I listened and explained that the situation would work itself out since he was less able to care for the pet. This sounded reasonable, but then she focused on visitation. She felt his visits disrupted her dog's behavior pattern.

This dog's behavior was never good. How on earth would she notice? Champ is a nasty crotch sniffer who humps everything he sees. That is what's happening here. People with no life focus on something and grasp onto it. For some, it's pets; for others, it's religion; and for some, it's gossip.

It ain't pets, and it ain't religion, so gossip must be my vice. I have slowly learned not to spread gossip—or at least to spread *less* gossip. But I just *love* to hear it. Other people's stories are fascinating. When people are more fucked up than I am, I get a warm feeling in my tummy. Call it superiority.

Later, I will share with you the worst gossip story I've got. Then I'll detail how the effects are still reverberating. I'll title that chapter, "Thank God I Never Slept with That Crazy Lesbian."

Lesson 17

GIVE CREDIT WHERE CREDIT IS DUE

JUNE 18, 2008

When Jackson and I met, neither of us had any interest in relationships. He was devastated that his wife left him after twenty years. The divorce papers came as a surprise to him, but anyone watching could have called it. He felt he'd raised her son and then got thrown out after the kid was ready for college. Damn, and I thought *I* was bitter! They had a shitty marriage, but that was all he knew. He was willing to do anything to make her change her mind, but his ex just said, "I'm done." He moved out, but he had not moved on.

I'd filled in the loneliness void with that lesser human being, Scammy. Darrin was always around, too. Scam and Darrin were driving me crazy, and I needed to escape before I killed them both. I spent the night at an Independence Day party I'd attended and asked Jackson if he wanted to lie down beside me. When I took his arm, wrapped it around me, and drifted off to sleep, he said he just knew. After that time, it seemed best to have him wrapped around me...or at least my little finger.

Later, he insisted on giving me a credit card. I handed it back, saying, "You should *never do this*! You should be very afraid."

"I need you to accept it," he replied. "It's up to you whether or not you use it."

It was all beautiful and meaningful until I asked, "So...what is our limit?"

JUNE 24, 2008

French toast with cinnamon butter and syrup. It's the little things in life that bring the most joy. Mmm, food can be a celebration in and of itself. And I partake, which means I am not a skinny bitch. One out of two ain't bad—I'm just simply a bitch. Cholesterol is a bit high, and flesh is a bit soft. Other than that, I am fit as a fiddle.

Fiddles and banjos remind me of home. This weekend, we went to my parents' house for our yearly family get-together—the one at my parents' place as opposed to the twentysomething other family get-togethers. For a family that is not very together, we sure get together a lot.

Why might one say that? We all have our own special form of crazy. Crazy is where I come from. I have the world's worst taste in men. Until now, I hope. Jayden, my sister, takes in foster kids with no regard to her own family. Dirk is a man-whore. Kit gets drunk and burns her child. Some refuse to wear a cage while playing hockey. Most of these are not truly horrifying but just teensy little bits of innocuous crazy.

After the drive home from Walnut Grove, it helps to have time to detox. But Sunday night, I chose to tox it up. Beer, whiskey—whatever ya got. Jax came with me to the "retreat," and he was kind enough to listen to my questions and validate my feelings. The questions were:

"The kid is two years old. Shouldn't he be speaking?"

"Do you think that one eats anything but fudge pops?"

"Why don't the kids put things in the trash can?"

"Do you think pulling the legs off the frog was a little excessive?"

Perfect mom I am not. But, dude! No wonder I have boundary issues! No wonder I have weight issues! We found bags of marshmallows in front of the television with only three left in it. Plastic children's drinks were strewn all over the yard. Kids were screaming for ice cream instead of breakfast, lunch, or dinner. And that was just my sister's brood.

My child is also imperfect. She loves me, of that there is no doubt. And she loves her food, too. She has separation anxiety and wants to be with her loving mother all the time. I hate to admit this, but the feeling is not mutual. I need my space. Summer has begun, and I will have no space. This concerns me.

My princess is a healthy eater. She's just a messy eater. Bring out the tarp and the hose. She does everything with her mouth open. Ugh! She forgets to eat over her plate. She forgets utensils. She forgets to chew. Monster Mommy is always there giving gentle but constant reminders.

When Jax listened to my tirade about the family, he changed the subject. He said sweet, loving things. He said his friends and family have watched him become a better man in the past couple of years, and he gave me the credit. Being with someone who loves, accepts, and supports him is nurturing. Being with someone who trusts is fortifying. Being with someone who is positive and humorous is energizing. Experiencing a healthy relationship is so incredibly rewarding after our experiences with our sullen, negative, soul-sucking exes. That said, there have been many times Jax has been poised to become another ex.

JULY 1, 2008

This weekend, I did the Relay For Life at Cornerstone College. It poured rain, and we had a postponement due to flash flooding. It was not my best weekend for physical activity, as my period did the same deluge thing. Hemorrhaging and running a relay do not mix. That part sucked. Losing three pints of blood is never good for the iron count. So, my energy level was a bit low. But I toughed it out as best I could. Translation: once you bleed through a series of outfits, ya'll should check yourself into the ER. Instead, I chose the white couch at home.

Then, somehow, I made it back out to an open house. Jax got to see his old friends from grade school. His friends have grown children. Only one or two of my friends have college-age kids. His friends are talking about hitting Hippie Fest. That's gonna be fun! Stacey is signed on, too!

Tonight I am hosting a sleepover for Ella and her friend, Stacey's daughter, Jennie. All they want to do is watch a video, and I am fully supportive. I called my boyfriend and talked dirty while the kids watched the video. Parenting can be fun, in moderation. Wonder if they will notice I am headed to bed before them?

JULY 7, 2008

I did get plenty of quality time with Jax at his place. He feels all loved and shit. I also feel all loved and shit, because he was intent on making sure I knew where he stands on the whole relationship thing. He is also aware of where I stand. When his brother was sitting up at the clubhouse bar with us, and he asked me what my intentions were with his little brother, Jackson, I immediately pulled out the deer-in-the-headlights look. He said, "Jackson and I have had a lot of talks, and I know where he stands on marriage" Okay, at this point, I take the large bottle of Jack sitting on the bar and start draining the bottle straight into my mouth. Both Jax's friends had to pry it from my hands, and Jax was saying, "Baby, it's okay. It's gonna be okay."

For the record, I apologized the next day, and my boy said he wouldn't change a thing. But I would. So, I initiated intense talks about money, kids, retirement, housing, drinking, smoking, gambling, debt, and in-laws. I think it will be a long time before those boys try to railroad me with silly questions again.

JULY 10, 2008

Angel's job is being eliminated, and her department will be replaced with a center in India. While she's waiting, I suggested she scrapbook in her cubicle and plan to take over the world. She'll get through. Chances are she'll have something lined up before the ax falls. I can bring a sledgehammer to trash office supplies that no one is shipping to India. Maybe we can do a remake of the smash-the-copier scene in *Office Space*. I got rid of my gun, so we can't shoot stuff off the back porch. But we can light stuff up and smash it to smithereens with my sledgehammer.

Eve's mother was over for dinner, and we found out that her family had a pet squirrel. Eve never mentioned this to me. Apparently she used to ride around with it on her shoulder. One day, it disappeared. Seems a neighbor in the Warren area had a hankering for squirrel.

Stacey's husband suggested I spray garlic all over my yard to keep the mosquitoes and deer from eating my hostas. Two years ago, I used moth balls. That reeked. Garlic just makes me think, "Mmm…pasta." At least I'm not thinking, "Mmm…possum or mmm squirrel."

On Tuesday, I have an interview with the bankrupt City of Pontiac. It's my best job lead so far.

JULY 14, 2008

This weekend, we hosted a pool party for a load of kids. There was no reason to have a party. There never needs to be a reason to have a party. It rained off and on, but we made it work. My loving boyfriend hosted this party at his place. As he was heading out to his own home to prep, Ella hugged him for the first time ever. She already has the holding-back-affection thing down. *Nice!* She will be a lovely wife someday.

Ella felt sorry for her dad, who was driving home alone, and asked if it was okay to go back to his place if we didn't have anything special planned that night. We gave the thumbs up. More orgasms for me! I'm going to Traverse City this weekend. Jack and I are leaving on Friday afternoon and coming home on Monday.

Lesson 18

CALL PEOPLE OUT ON THEIR SHIT

JULY 21, 2008

Jax, his friends, and I just spent the weekend in Traverse City. It was a good time. Now, I was again ambushed regarding the relationship thing—the second time I have been ambushed in a matter of weeks. Maybe Jackson has some super-secret feelings regarding this issue. This time a five-year-old set me up.

JULY 22, 2008

We got back from Traverse City last night. This little missy had never driven a Jet Ski before. Jack rode on the back while I drove. We hung out at the beautiful beach house belonging to his friend Bryce's family. Bryce's mom is so worried that he will never find a well-mannered young lady of proper breeding. Mick's wife, Jill, didn't make his mom feel any better when she explained that her son simply doesn't speak to girls. Jill tried setting him up and was completely frustrated by his indifference. I tried introducing him to some ladies too, and he wasn't talking to them. Who needs romance anyway, right?

Okay, maybe I do. It's growing on me. I got a lot of it, what with walks on the beach and bonfires. Jax made a cute message designed in seashells on the sand for me, and I took pictures. Nothing risqué, just our names with a little heart and arrow, but it made me warm and fuzzy. We were so cutesy that when we went walking along the beach, everyone was speculating on our future. Speculation is cool. The part where they set up a five-year-old to ask, "Jack? So, do you think you're going to marry Jewel?" was less cool. Yes, I ran to the liquor cabinet—again. We need a new shtick. When I reentered the room, I showed the kid my promise ring. At that point, Jax said, "Yeah, it is a promise ring. I promised not to bring up marriage." It keeps coming up, and I am running out of material.

JULY 29, 2008

Today, I am playing Queen of Hades to my demon spawn. My demon spawn is sometimes a pig, just like her father. There are piles of hair in CARB's house bigger than my thigh. You trip over them. Ironically, he owns a robot vacuum. All you do is push a button, and the thing cleans up for you. Is it really too damn hard to push a button?

There are dead bugs in his home the size of my foot. That begs the question, exactly how big are the live ones? The ones that survived? Does a large spider spring out from a dark corner and suck the life out of them? Is this why pushing a button on a robot vacuum takes so much effort? The spiderwebs here are quite large. I hope the super-sized arachnid waits for my alimony to be up before it sucks what little life is left out of the semihuman who owes it to me.

The ex gets credit for watching movies with my child and for taking her boating on my old boat. He does not get any credit whatsoever for teaching her manners. That's because he's a pig. As I write, my spawn is eating lunch. Slowly but surely, she's trying to eat more quietly. She's slowly but surely trying to eat over the table and the plate. She's slowly learning to swallow before she shovels in another mouthful. This behavior horrifies me. The only person it bothers more is my ex-step-monster-in-law. Catherine takes great pains to point out all my daughter's flaws.

Goodness knows she did the same thing to me. She was appalled at everything I said or did. I never fit her image of what befitted the Cohen name. Yet *she* was the little tramp picked up at the Vic Tanny's juice bar. *She* was the one who used to live out of her van with her loser boyfriend when they couldn't make it in the music business. *She's* the one who never made it through college. But my daughter and I are somehow not good enough.

When the kid comes back from visiting, she's often in tears. Ella wants to know why Nana says the mean things she does, because they hurt her feelings. My response is always that I am sorry and that Nana did not mean to hurt her. She doesn't know much about kids. My internal response is, "Nana knows nothing about feelings. She is too high and too numb to feel anything. Her feelings were buried long ago when she sold her soul to the devil to get her cushy, rich-bitch lifestyle back."

JULY 31, 2008

As long as I've ranted about that one bitch, let's go back to pets for a moment. My friend Angelique's dog, Bennie, was diagnosed with lymphoma. She is beside herself. It is incurable. But she is buying him time at $500 a pop for chemo. When I was growing up, my family would have popped him with a slug.

Still, I hate to see Angelique hurting. Love is love. The color, gender, religion, and species are unimportant. My tongue has turned to hamburger from biting it so much. The only right thing to do is be supportive. Anything less seems unfeeling. I do give a crap, I really do. But I am angry.

You see, Angelique is obsessing over her pet's having cancer, and it consumes her. McKenna is out of remission with lymphoma. A human, one of my favorite humans, has the same form of cancer—the second time around!

Mac acknowledges the prayers and the well-wishers. She keeps us informed of her progress. The cancer is back. I am horrified and powerless. Mac is horrified and powerless. All she can do is wait and see how soon the cells mutate into something deadly.

My anger is not about the pets. It never has been. And it's not with Angel. It's about losing the things you love. You expect a pet to go before you, because that is the nature of most creatures we choose as pets. You know this information going in.

Knowing that I may have to live my life without Mac is scary. When I hurt and need a shoulder, she is on the short list. When I have a job interview, I call her. After therapy, I call her. When I was ready to have a nervous breakdown, when I gave birth, when I got divorced, she was there. This woman means the world to me. She is my sister in a way my blood sister could never be.

AUGUST 4, 2008

When we were married, Darrin had vertigo and took Valium, which helped some. His vertigo was said to be caused by stress. I guess it must be stressful to be such an ass. Now, Angel has vertigo too. She's been unable to get rid of it. But I know someone who has a simple fix. Jack has a friend named Ken, whom we call Vertigo Ken. He has no warning as to when it would come on, which is scary. He was unable to drive home from a party at Jack's place, so I took him home. Turns out it was his eyesight that caused the problem. When he had glasses made (contacts wouldn't work) with an extra line that helped him focus, there was no more vertigo. He teaches spin classes (c'mon, that's funny), so glasses are a pain—but it worked. If Angel hasn't had her eyes checked, it's worth a shot.

This Sunday was Jackson-and-Jewel day. He'd been asking for time alone to do whatever *we* wanted. Well, I wanted to go to Home Depot. Then we went to sit at his pool. Hippie Fest was fun. We had a pool party earlier in the day, and my buzz lasted all day and all night. Buzz might be too light a term. Anyway, people said I had fun. I was blowing bubbles and dancing while the boyfriend babysat me this time as opposed to my child.

Now I'm back to being all responsible and shit. I made strawberry shortcake this weekend with fat-free whipped cream and sugar-free glaze. Jack will be having a party at his place since I'm unavailable. I was very disappointed that he would have a sausage fest without me. All those hockey players in the pool and no Jewel to witness it is sad. He told me to just enjoy my clit fest and that he'd see me on Sunday.

I was grilled again regarding my intentions with Jax. If he's going to let his friends and family disturb me, then he's going to have to babysit my drunk ass. My whole family is the complete opposite. They just act as if nothing is happening. They don't ask how he is and pretend that I have no special person in my life. They don't really act like I am special either, come to think of it.

My neighbor Kylie asks more questions, and we speak every six months. Tonight we spoke regarding her dog's shit. I wrote a lovely letter explaining my feelings about her dogs crapping in my yard on a daily basis. This letter was written after I piled the crap on her front step and other assorted places. She said she wished I had called earlier. I said I wished she had asked herself where the dog crap goes every day. The answer, I told her, was, "My yard—in the morning, at night when you come home, and every other time you let them out. For example, you get the mail, and your dog shits in my yard as you walk into your house." In the end, she said she would get an invisible fence and we would be done with the issue. Here's my note:

> Hi, Kylie,
>
> It looks like you were making more of an effort to keep your dogs out of my yard for a little while. Thanks. The effort was appreciated. We have been over this before. I have asked you to clean up the dog poop after you let them do their business in my yard. You are a smart, responsible person, and this behavior doesn't fit who you are. Some options you may not have considered would be invisible fencing, leashing both animals, or finding new homes for them.
>
> Your next-door neighbor,
> Jewel

What I really wanted to do was dump a truckload of manure on her driveway, but I stopped just short. She has excuses, such as she's busy running a triathlon, her friend has cancer, fences seemed expensive, and she thought I liked dogs. My condo association must have some kind of policy for this.

AUGUST 8, 2008

Today is my sister's birthday. We'll drive over to visit. Oh, and another close friend, Sandee, is losing her dog, Patches, to cancer. This is why my rants are nonverbal. I feel for my friends; I do. I just can't get there in my head.

My stress level is up. The good news is that people are responding to my job applications. I'm doing a couple of interviews per week. Still, the only offers

I've received have been for jobs that would not even begin to pay the bills. No wonder generations of people live off the social welfare system.

Yesterday I had a good meeting with a solid company. We know the salary is in line, and the job could be done. It would be an exciting opportunity, too. New beginnings? Maybe.

Jax came over in the evening. Our relationship has progressed. The rose-colored glasses are fading to a light pink. Light pink as in "sometimes my girlfriend embarrasses me."

Yesterday, Ella and I went to Jackson's house, and he made us dinner. We spent the night, and he said he was thrilled to have us. The following morning, we ate what little food we could find in the bachelor pad out on the patio. There we saw his daughter and her friend, who had biked over. Being a good little mommy, I asked the kids in. They found one more kid and then spent the day at the pool. We made lunch and had an enjoyable day. That is, until some nasty old biddy came along and bitched at the kids while I was upstairs washing the last of the dishes. I came downstairs and waited for her to come out of the pool house. She didn't come out, so I went into the office and introduced myself. And this is where the fun began. The conversion went as follows:

"Hi, my name is Jewel Cohen. I am the responsible adult at the pool. I heard you were concerned. Would you like to share your concerns with another adult?"

GK (stands for Gladys Kravitz): Who are you?

JC (for Jewel Cohen and also Jesus Christ, because I am that righteous): Again, my name is Jewel. Jewel Cohen. Now that we've got that, this is the part where you say your name.

GK: I've never seen you before.

JC: I disagree. You most certainly have. You live directly under Melvin. Is that correct?

GK: Yes.

JC: Okay. Then you would be the woman who is always staring at me. You walk out your door and stare for a full two minutes, and then I wave and say hello. That's because it is impolite to stare, and it kinda creeps people out. Well, I am so pleased to have satisfied your curiosity. What else do you need to know?

GK (picture the dude on *Office Space* who was fired but they kept him on the payroll—the one with stapler issues—but slightly more feminine, or if you are a bit older, the nosy neighbor from *Bewitched*): I'm Gladys. Do you live here? I know the rules. You haven't read them, but I know them, and you can't be here.

JC (proceeds to pick a copy of the rules off the desk and read her the rules verbatim): In addition, I know there is an association board, and I would suggest that you go to the board and discuss this with them to see if you are the only one concerned. Should you find anyone else who wishes to waste our time, the board can vote or put a vote out to the association residents. I am aware that each unit is allowed one vote, yada, yada, blah, blah...

GK: I am concerned about the safety of the children.

JC (at this point, I am concerned about GK's safety, because drowning her dumb ass sounds like a really good idea): Really? Yes, we do need to obey safety rules, such as the ones I mentioned. I own a home in Pleasant Ridge. My child and I are often here, also. Jackson also has a child who lives here. If it makes a difference to anyone important, my name will be added to the lease. Are we done here?

GK: I don't know you.

JC: You obviously do not. Why don't you go talk to someone who does and get back to me? Gladys, who is on your board?

GK proceeds to name them and says that no one else is in town. Charming that she knows everyone's whereabouts.

JC: Gladys, I've been around for two years. I will be outside this door on a lounge chair if there are any further problems you need my assistance with.

GK: What did you say your name is?

JC: My name is Jewel, and yours is Gladys.

Well, that went well. Except for the boyfriend—saying that I'm abrasive and shit. Seriously, he has the audacity to say that I don't always make things better when I walk in to straighten things out. So, that's why I'm sleeping alone tonight. Thanks, Gladys, you dumb cunt! I feed the kids and entertain the children, and this is the thanks I get. That's it. There's no need to go to the old folks' home ever again. He can come here when he's ready to apologize and admit that I am the sweetest, kindest soul he has ever met! In the meantime, I'm proving my loving kindness by staging a death match with my own neighbor whose dog craps in my yard and his nosy neighbor.

Jackson was not even present but was positive I did not make things better by chatting with Gladys. Now, is that any way to treat a teammate? He described me as sometimes being a little overly aggressive. Now, I am politely demeaning, but rarely out-and-out abrasive. If people would just know their place and keep to it, I wouldn't have to politely remind them.

There's a slight chance I'm more stressed than usual and just itching for a fight. There may have been another heated discussion with one of my neighbors. Again, if people weren't out-of-control stupid, we would never be having these conversations. Kinda dumb people are funny and make us feel better about our own stupid mistakes. Being so ignorant that people want to kill you, though, is a dangerous thing.

A local recruiter I know is so ignorant I want to put her head on the pavement and smash it. I've lost that loving feeling, because people who don't know how to spell their own name have paying jobs and I don't. People who don't have the sense to brush their teeth work in sales positions.

So, how fucked up does that make me? This girl is bitter. Bitter, bitter, bitter. I worry and obsess. The lines in my forehead are deepening. *Tick-tock*—alimony is running out. Unemployment is a small but helpful check that will soon run out. I wake up with headaches. Can I not just work up to a headache like other people rather than wake up to one?

AUGUST 11, 2008

Maybe this girl has anger-management issues. The visit back to the west side of the state went well. Jax and Amy had been invited, but it worked out even better without them.

Ella and I came over to the family compound on Friday afternoon. We stopped at McDonald's on the way and were still there by three. I missed my parents. We may never "get" each other, but we are a family and love one another. We went boating and swimming Friday evening. Saturday was spent doing a little shopping and more boating. We fed fish and turtles in a pretty little homemade bass pond and then had a bonfire and a sleepover. Sunday was fort-making day. The girls and one extra blond kid used eighteen blankets to build a fort that spanned half the first level. We ate lunch downstairs because the fort had expanded so far.

My mom loves being a grandma. One cannot help but love Rhett Thomas. Rhett couldn't look any less similar to his family if he tried. Jayden's girls are all white skin, white hair, and light eyes. They are languid. They watch television, eat marshmallows, and suck their thumbs much of the day.

Rhett has dark skin, dark hair, and dark eyes. He is two years old and faster than a speeding bullet. Rhett is one kid I understand. He has two speeds: stop and go. He runs everywhere and climbs everything. Rhett is all boy and all action.

Some children take a moment to warm up to others. When Rhett first sees me after an absence, he sizes me up. I respect that. It's as if he's saying, "You look like my mommy. You smell like my mommy. You are so *not* my mommy!" Jayden has been his mommy since the beginning. Rhett was given a life he never would have had with his allegedly ghetto-dwelling, crack-smoking, whoring birth mother.

Jax did get a letter from his condo association restating the pool rules. There's no rule against Amy or myself at the pool if we are listed as residents. This place has never in its history had a minor listed as a resident. So, the board will have to look at the policy and decide how best to proceed. Jax did not back down, and I'm proud of him for that.

The part that disturbed me was that he automatically assumed I'd done the wrong thing. That behavior comes with baggage. My family does not ask about my relationships because they can't help but cringe. Just this weekend, I reported on another interview, and my father cringed twice in a row. Finding out how many times I can make the parents cringe has become a game for me. The bar in their household is pretty high; it's amazing what you have to say and do to get a reaction.

Still, my inability to secure a lasting career is my most glaring fault. I try so hard and see no results. So, having my father look at me with the "you did not just say that" face was withering.

This is probably why we discuss nothing of substance. We all judge one another harshly. Families often give more respect to homeless people than the people they share their home with. Going through old family photos reminds me of the sacrifices my parents made. They still make sacrifices to this day to assure their children's health and happiness. We're gonna be okay. I promise. Last night, Jax, Ella, and I danced in the living room. Those moments are precious and fleeting. I love my life.

AUGUST 12, 2008

Ward and Eve came over last night, as they're having their bathroom redone and there's only one bathroom in their home. Eve gave Jax her opinion on the DC story. It was pretty much, "Jewel is your teammate—you *have* to back her." He called the board president, and they spoke at length. In addition, he spent time with his daughter and realizes that I'm just supporting our kids. Oh…and I'm the one who apologized for any trouble this may cause him, although I haven't yet received an apology from him.

Lesson 19

SMILE AND PRETEND
THINGS ARE SWELL

AUGUST 16, 2008

Yesterday, we did the waterpark with Ella and a bunch of kids. Today, I will be boating with Ward and Eve. Later on, I'll hit the Woodward Dream Cruise. There's a beer tent at the American Legion, a barbeque at Jackson's beforehand, and then some fun with the guys.

Tomorrow will be fun with the girls at ChickFest. CARB just grabbed Ella to take her up north last night. She probably slept the whole way up. These breaks are wonderful. Shit, I never got five minutes to myself when I was married. Now I have three-day weekends!

AUGUST 18, 2008

What a fantastic weekend! I'm thinking I wouldn't mind if Jax had a low-libido issue this week. Can these things swell shut? If so, mine might be starting to.

The chicks are the kind of people I'd love to grow old with. Maybe we are getting a little tamer. Pretty soon we'll have to start partying at six to make it past nine. Who cares? We rock!

My chocolates got polished off last night. That's just not the kind of stuff I need to share with my kid. On the sharing issue, everyone added something special, like the house and boat, food, DVD presentation, drinks, hats, photos, listening skills, music, and comedy. It was so fun to reflect yesterday. Life is good.

AUGUST 19, 2008

Pneumonia sucks. This girl has been hospitalized for it. Sandee's husband, Newman, has it. Boys can be whiny-ass bitches when they have the sniffles. From my experience, bells do not work—and do not give a sick man a phone or intercom. My stupid ex constantly asked me for obnoxious shit when he was in bed sick.

I did add some new things to the adult toy chest. Some items wore out, and some were intimidating. If you need to gas it up and pull-start it before use, some dudes just turtle up…speaking of whiny-ass bitches.

AUGUST 20, 2008

News on the latest job opportunity! That would be bad news…again. The official statement is that they're changing the criteria and are now looking for someone with a background heavy in training. That's it…I'm going to go sell drugs in Pontiac. That will be convenient for my new home at Grace Centers of Hope. I can get clothes at the Hidden Treasures Resale Shop they run. See, I have a plan for our future.

Okay, my real plan is to tell the recruiters that my part-time position is ending and that I am completely available for anything full-time and local over ten dollars an hour. It's a fire sale, and I'm going for half price. I'll do home-improvement projects and wait until Ella goes back to school on September 2 before I make any major plans. I'm getting much better at home repairs. In the meantime, I have maybe one or two stones left unturned job-wise.

AUGUST 26, 2008

ChickFest was a blast, boating was relaxing, and the Dream Cruise was fun, too. Life is not all bad. But somehow I don't remember removing my clothes the night of the Dream Cruise. Those are the nights I'm glad I have a steady boyfriend. He's quick to assure me that I had a wonderful time. What may have put me over the top was the whiskey in the thirty-two-ounce Super Big Gulp.

The following day, pulling it together to hang with the girls was imperative. There would be no hangover excuses. I was tough—I made it. Sandee had to explain to some of us that the pickled pineapple vodka was a sipping drink and not something to gulp down. I mixed lemonade with it so as not to get dehydrated on the boat.

Remember when as kids we used to be afraid of the cops? Not anymore. Now, my friends and I are the upstanding citizens who call them when we need something. I called to alert them to my dock squatter last summer. In that case, response did not come in a timely manner, so I handled it myself.

At the Downtown Hoedown, I'd found an officer or two and asked them to have a chat with a dirty little whore who had poured beer on several people, including myself. And for ChickFest, one agreeable gentleman in uniform ran up to the store to get us some ice. Running out of ice is an emergency. He offered to assist us, and we provided some entertainment on his lake. It's comforting to know that as a respectable citizen, you've got people in uniform watching out for you.

I will only ask for help if I cannot take care of something myself. I am not Corrine. Corrine is a SAHM with two kids who orders her husband around. He works all day at EDS and comes home to face her to-do list. She signs him up as coach, has him do the kid's homework with them, and sends him out to do all the shopping.

Corrine does not see herself as demanding; it's just her right as a spouse. She's fun to debate with, because the idea that she could be wrong has never occurred to her. She, too, has been known to contact people in uniform for help. She's the neighbor you love to hate who calls the city regarding sound ordinances, kids walking down the street looking suspicious, and people driving either too fast or too slow in her subdivision.

She recently called the neighbor about the kid's radio in the driveway and asked that it be turned off or tuned down. He was listening while playing basketball at one o'clock in the afternoon. I might have supported her if it was one in the morning, but one in the afternoon? C'mon.

Now, I go after stupid people only when I must. Okay…and maybe some-times as sport. But I try to choose my battles. So, when she gave me a war story about fighting with a fifth grader, I had to tell her that was overboard. And if *I* say something is overboard, that's code for *out of control*!

Amy turned fifteen yesterday. There will be a party this weekend at Jackson's place. I was disappointed last August, because it felt strange to be celebrating at his ex's house with all family and one girlfriend. He left me alone with the certifiably crazy sister-in-law who was doing her best to create tension. There was no need for her to create tension. I'd walked in with it.

I've been taking Ella to appointments to get her ankle checked out. She sprained it playing on a trampoline at my cousin's house. The fat kid might have fallen on it. The swelling hasn't gone down, and it looks bad. So, I went to the pediatrician and had it X-rayed, and they called back to say it looked fine but then went over it again and said maybe there *was* a problem. So, I then met with an orthopedic specialist, who looked at the X-ray and her ankle and decided it was a sprain. Maybe my parents had the right idea when they never took me to the doctor. Of course, her swelling would go down faster if Darrin didn't refuse to ice it. Nope, Darrin won't ice it, because Jack gave us advice on how to handle the injury, and he makes special ice packs. Darrin needed this to be a sprain so that he could save face. He's always been jealous of Jax, especially when it comes to our kid.

AUGUST 27, 2008

My interview today ended with, "I plan to call you back in for a second inter-view, but I fear you are overqualified." *Grrrr!*

Dammit! Sandee's husband, Newman is getting laid off. Thank goodness this isn't a recession (I say in a bitchy, sarcastic voice). Sandee made a good call not marrying a loser. Damn, I shoulda made the same call. Newman is a good guy and he adores Sandee.

Sandee's first fiancé was a cheater. Cheaters deserve bad rashes. Well, most of them. I sorta technically qualify, but I didn't do anything until after the papers were served. Still, I could have waited the whole seven months. No...I could not have. Sex is very important for stress relief, and people would have died.

I am skipping a camping trip with my family to attend two functions for Jack's. Ella and I will head to his place tonight to swim and drink wine. Only one of the girls will drink wine.

Lesson 20

STORMS TEACH YOU TO SAIL

AUGUST 28, 2008

It's a dark, rainy morning. Dark, reflecting my mood. Yesterday I had yet another interview. Yet another interview where the interviewer states how much they like me, how smart I am, and how amazingly professional—and yet does not offer me the job. And, of course, there's always the usual, "You are overqualified." So, I am just too much. Too smart, too pretty, too ambitious, and too educated.

One person in my life I was not too much for: my ex-husband. To him, I was never enough. What about a nice, happy medium? Sometimes I'm too much for Jackson. But he can take it. He's an ex-marine, for God's sake. He can handle a little girl.

Last night, Jackson accused me of doing too much for dinner. That's ironic, considering I used to cook for Seven-Course Darrin. Anyway, Jackson instituted a new rule: in his home, there will be premade meals or hot dogs. His rule is based on the theory that his home should be viewed as a summer cottage or dorm room.

Last night was not the best night to repeatedly tell me I do too much. Near the end of the month, nothing should be said without first offering a piece of chocolate. Besides, I only made Chinese dumplings, rice, veggies, shrimp, sauce, and soup. That wasn't bad. It's not like I'm compulsive or anything.

SEPTEMBER 1, 2008

Labor Day. The only one I see laboring is my pool boy, Jax. He's skimming the pool. We did the party thing with Amy's, Jack's nephew's, plus Ward and Eve's parties. Taking Friday night off was a good call.

Speaking of calling, I called Ella while she was vacationing with her father—again. She's been busier than I've been. This weekend she went to Chicago. She hit the Sears Tower, American Girl doll store, Navy Pier, and goodness knows what else. This was all after they took a road trip to Ann Arbor to eat at the Blue Nile. Never mind the fact there's a Blue Nile in Ferndale, just up Woodward. That's too easy.

Next up, they'll hit the Renaissance Festival, the state fair, and then Alaska. And I was only going to take her to play miniature golf. If I want to get out of the golf game, I'll just suggest that Jackson and Ella planned a day together that includes golf. Then the ex will have to kick it up a notch and take her to Pebble Beach. Oh, the Alaska thing was an exaggeration. He might try Pebble Beach.

SEPTEMBER 5, 2008

We'll have to come up with something good for Angelique's fiancé's birthday gift that does not include inappropriate adult toys, such as the smother box. Is there really an "appropriate" adult toy, come to think of it?

I had two interviews this week. Both had stupidly low pay, were a bit of a drive, and offered less than twenty-five hours per week. Mac gave me a good lead, but the employer seemed to have changed her mind regarding full-time work after she put the order in to the agency. The other person is self-employed, has never hired anyone for her business before, has no furniture, and is hoping for someone to take over. Unemployment does not pay well, but it pays better than either of these. Maybe I'll just stain the decks.

Here's my thank-you letter to one of the employers. I knew I was not getting the job. I could drink a fifth of vodka in the morning and still do more than these people need. It is insanely frustrating and a colossal waste of time and effort.

Here's what the letter said:

Dear Mr. H——,

Thank you for interviewing me on Wednesday morning. It was a pleasure to meet you. Congratulations on the upcoming birth of your fourth child! How exciting.

Your assessment of my skills is the exact same response I am getting from every potential employer. My knowledge of the current job market and under-standing of personal finance lead me to believe this would be a good opportunity. In other words, I would hate to have to sling burgers for a living because I am too overqualified to obtain something in my field.

Again, I appreciate your time and am grateful to have had the opportunity to meet you.

Sincerely,

Jewel Cohen

To top off my day, Ella has opted to be a whiny little cretin—the kind of whiny little monster that tells you you're playing the board game all wrong after you've spent most of the night reading a Nancy Drew mystery to her, making her a nutritious dinner, planning a sleepover, and talking over girl stuff. If she were to sleep in my bed tonight, I'm afraid I'd accidentally smother her with my pillow. Oops…she just walked up behind me, and I accidentally taught her to read. Shit!

Lesson 21

SCARE PEOPLE

SEPTEMBER 12, 2008

Yesterday I had a cattle-call interview. I already got an e-mail from them saying, "No, thank you." The issue wasn't my references this time, because we didn't get that far. The company, called Mega Dog, sells dog-training tapes, among other things. I wasn't holding out much hope as they seemed iffy to begin with. For example, I got a call on Saturday asking if I could group interview on Monday. I couldn't do it and suggested a reschedule. At the reschedule, the caller, Colleen, asked about my salary requirements, and I said I was open to any reasonable opportunity. She said, "You would be willing to learn the ropes and start from the ground up?" I guess that depends on what bottom feeders are paid these days.

So, I go to this interview, which is held in a glorified warehouse. There are stalls downstairs and one loft-like office upstairs. I am the first person there, so I occupy myself by adding things to the to-do list. You know, the things I *could* be doing instead of being here with these morons. Anyway, I start to talk to the others as they come in. They are all twice the woman I am (in pound-age, at least). One has quit her job with no backup plan. The other was let go by Chrysler.

They start the interview by saying, "We'd like you to interview us." Well, that's easy. My questions were simple: "How would you prefer to be addressed?"

and "What did you do before this?" They did okay on the first question, but my concerns grew when the answer to the second question was, "I trained dogs before I became a puppet for the man in the nice office. Now I'm president of a new division, and we treat everyone like family here." Another was a zoologist before she became the operations manager.

Then they mentioned that the interview process is unconventional, and people have been known to walk out of the interview numerous times. The interview process was set up as a series of tasks. The first task assigned after the reverse interview was to take an object out of your purse and set it on the table. I wished I had come packing a gun so that I could slap a nine millimeter on the table and say, "No one is walking out of this interview." My other option was pulling out a tampon, but I couldn't decide between light and super. So, I opted for the extra strap on my purse.

The next step was to describe this object, tell why it holds value, and sell it to the interviewees. Uh…are you for real? One lady did not carry a purse, so they asked her to describe her favorite hobby. The fat, dumb bitch probably sat on her purse, and it was stuck somewhere in her folds. For the record, her hobby was taking pictures of inanimate objects that she would hope to sell. They asked for a volunteer, so I let the heavy smoker go next. God forbid I seem too aggressive. She pulled out a family photo and tried to sell it. Did I mention these were really ugly kids? Did I also mention that they gave us the option of picking out something different once we knew we'd have to sell it? No one wants to purchase a photo of ugly children. No one wants to purchase ugly children, for that matter.

Huh. I was told I had to go next because the dog walker needed to know what my object was. He was enthralled. Wouldn't he want to know what I could do with a leather strap? I explained it was an additional strap that came with my purse. It was as yet unused, but it showed that I was always prepared and organized. Then I went on to describe the different uses these two morons would have for my strap. While doing so, I snapped it to prove the strap's strength. Some potential uses would be a leash for pets, a harness for small children in overcrowded and dangerous situations, and a handy key holder. The key holder would be especially helpful for an elderly relative who tends to lose things. Who does *not* know someone with children, older relatives, or pets? This strap is a vital tool that everyone should carry.

Another question was, "Do you definitively know the origin of the phrase *the whole nine yards?*" I didn't raise my hand on that one, either. We could get the answer by asking yes or no questions. Once again, I let the others ask their questions, which included, "Like, are you talking material?" The dog walker told me I could keep asking questions and didn't have to wait for the others. He was patronizing and scoffed at the ignorant questions. I reminded the group (in my cheerleader voice) that there was no such thing as a stupid question and that we should keep going until we solve the mystery. We solved it. The origin of the quote refers to artillery in WWII. There were nine yards of ammo, and if you used all nine yards, you'd given it all you had.

This isn't all. I have one more story. On my way home from this interview, I spoke with Darrin. He was upset because he was having a problem with stickers. I said, "Listen, I am two minutes from your place. I'll stop in." You had to see this to believe it. I bring an example with me everywhere I go. He bought these cheapo little testing kits from 3M. Then he marked them up 400 percent and pasted a sticker on them with his name on it. Now, the trouble is that the stickers are removable…and so cheap that the edges beg for you to tear them off. So, when the clients/purchasers get their marked-up merchandise, they'll see they've been duped. Then they'll simply buy directly from 3M and use the savings to pay someone to kill Darrin. So, let's go over this: he buys something on the cheap, puts a "Hello, My Name Is" sticker over it, and sells it as his own at an outrageous price. Then he wonders why he gets no repeat business. Yet this dude has a job and I do not—as does the dog walker, zoologist, and numerous people who do not have the mental capacity of a toad.

When I whined to Jack, he said, "Baby, you scare people." I knocked back a shot and said, "They are a bunch of pussies. Fuck 'em."

My anger stems from a complete lack of control over the future. My friend Hailey, the funeral director, always says it best when dealing with life or death, partly because that's her business, and partly because she's simply wiser than

I am. Here are her thoughts regarding the big, black cloud hanging over the people who love Mac:

Yeah, she's scared (who wouldn't be?), but Mac doesn't often vocalize the fear part (at least, she never has with me). She seems to adopt an "it is what it is" attitude, at least on the outside. Ten years ago, she downplayed ultimate negative outcomes and dealt only in facts. Everything happened very fast, and before we knew it, she had her surgical biopsies and was dealt the bad news. Then, before we knew it, she was hooked up with the doctor in Ann Arbor and doing the experimental treatment that thankfully worked so well for these past ten years.

In the back of all our minds (including Mac's) is the worst-case scenario. It pops into our brains, and then we push it away, because a positive attitude leads to a stronger will and a healthier mind and body to fight this thing. We also know that if those around her are positive, it helps her be positive and strong. So easy to say and to type, but we will do it.

Then there are those moments when you/me/us/Mac aren't feeling so confident. Those moments suck…and I'm sorry, but I'm in one right now. I know it could very well be a roller-coaster ride these next few months or years as far as treatments, remissions, successes, emotions, frustrations, hospital stays, and so on.

I'm also angry at the moment. I have no doubt she has angry moments, too. Unfortunately, I'll bet it gets redirected toward the one person she can and does get pissed at occasionally. That would be you, Moe, as she's with you at some point every day. What do you do? Admit you're afraid, too? How do you deal with the irritability she no doubt is experiencing? Couple the lymphoma with what is happening in her employment world, and there's no way she doesn't snap regularly. My role…our role as her friends will always be different than yours, and it will differ between each of us, as we all know Mac on a different level.

Moe, just be there for her. When she gets bitchy and irritable, just try grabbing her and hugging her. If she pushes you away…damn it, just hold on harder.

SEPTEMBER 14, 2008

Jax was concerned that I'm spending less time with my friends. I told him to shut up and keep pouring us drinks Friday night. That may not have been supportive.

I found a slug on the sidewalk, and I almost took it home and named it Darrin. I stopped short because I couldn't handle the slime trail. The best part was that my slug was outside Bob Evans. Darrin used to eat sausage gravy at Bob Evans and moan on the couch for the rest of the day. Those were our weekends in a nutshell, as we didn't get out much. So, there's no need for Soldier Boy's concern. I get out a lot more now than I used to when I was married.

I'm pushing forward with the state of Michigan and their NWLB Act (No Worker Left Behind). Many other acts, such as the Displaced Homemakers Self-Sufficiency Assistance Act, are kinda rolled into one now. Anyway, looks like I may qualify. People who qualify can take classes in growing fields in Michigan. That leaves truck driving and health care—unless I'm missing something. We don't want me behind the wheel of a big rig, and no real childcare is available for people who travel. Nannies don't really travel with you on those things. That leaves health care, and OCC has a campus up the street. A little state funding, maybe a Pell Grant, and whatever work I can find in order to squeak by may provide a light at the end of the tunnel that isn't a train.

Or…I can be a roofer. Roofers are listed as a growing field in Michigan—along with HR positions. I can smoke pot and swear, and I don't need no edumacac-hun. Yep—roofer it is.

SEPTEMBER 17, 2008

My hands are all grass stained, and the sweat is pouring down. This morning it was job search, bill pay, and vacation planning. Included in there were mixed garage cleanup and lawn mowing. The lawn is over halfway done.

This weekend, we may play laser tag at Jennie's birthday party, go to another birthday sleepover, maybe see Cheech and Chong at the Fillmore, go boating, and hit a little Hebrew School.

Ella will be doing school at the Jewish Community Center. All I ask is that less than 50 percent of the participants are not atheist. Also, it's best if the congregants are not haters. Class is from 10:15 a.m. to 12:15 p.m. every Sunday. At the Birmingham Temple, her Sunday school teachers were practic-ing atheists.

Now, how can I pull off church, too? This mama got the easy out. Good luck on your personal spiritual journey, princess—Mama's having coffee in bed with her man. Jackson is thrilled.

This weekend, I would have to leave the sleepover frighteningly early to get her to class. Yuck. She and I will be cranky. If I get a free ticket to Cheech and Chong, that will seal the deal. We'd stay home. Let me rephrase. She would stay home, and I would go out. Jackson is free and volunteered to watch Ella so I can go out. Where is Darrin, my usual sitter? He will be at a pig roast. Does anyone else see the irony? He is a pig, and most people assume he won't eat pork. The pork is free; he will eat it.

I fell for Jax after a series of Sunday mornings holding hands at church. Now, he is giving up a Saturday night to help out Darrin, Ella, and me. Darrin was undaunted. He's invited out rather infrequently. Go figure. When he said he would stay home, I told him we'd come up with a better plan.

I've had some crazy interviews lately, and I'm toying with the idea of going back to school. Six months of unemployment is insane! I've been to agencies, applied all over, and networked my heart out. My laundry room, closets, toolbox, furnace room, kitchen, and garage are all reorganized. Oh...but there's more mowing. Here I go...

Lesson 22

KEEP MOVING—YOU ARE LAPPING EVERYONE ON THE COUCH

SEPTEMBER 19, 2008

Lester, a former employee of one of my old firms, called last night and sent me on an interview this afternoon. They want me to start Monday. The company is in robotics, and the position is sales administration representative. I used the "Jewel Lite" resume, and we took off my master's degree. Lester suggested that I "be blond." *Nice.* But it worked. They want to on a temp-to-perm basis.

SEPTEMBER 24, 2008

I've made it through the first three days, and they haven't pulled me into the office for "the talk" yet. I'm still shell shocked from the crazy bullshit of the last couple years. This job is temp to perm, and they do need the help. This is a multinational corporation, and there is no beer machine and no Cruella. What I *do* have is a horrible cold. You know, the kind that makes your head fuzzy, and you get dizzy when you blow your nose (or is that just me?). My child tucked me into bed at seven thirty last night. Holy shit! Tonight, Darrin went to her curriculum night, and I stayed with Ella and the dog.

The teachers seem to have backed off on the hour and a half of homework per night. Oh, sure...the kids get a good MEAP score—my pleasure. I'll be sending the bill at the end of the month to account for the extra assistance I have put in to achieve this result.

I'm fortunate to have landed something in this sucky economy, and I will do all I can to keep it. This means that if something has to give, I'll let the homework slide. Grades don't really count up until high school, anyway.

SEPTEMBER 28, 2008

Yeah, baby! A Sunday afternoon in bed is even better than Sunday morning. My boyfriend is all snuggled up next to me. We toyed with the idea of canoeing. Now is the time to insert the joke about the little man in the canoe. But no, that was too easy.

Really, I'm just trying to be all positive. When I climbed into bed, I was nearly crying. As luck would have it, enough phlegm is coming up while coughing to fill a mason jar, feminine difficulties are occurring, breathing is labored, and a diabetic coma was narrowly escaped. At least it's not mono again. Is a working body too much to ask?

The good news is, this body is working. Of course, on Monday morning, the fever kicked into high gear. But there was no way in hell I was calling in to work. So, while I should have checked into the hospital, I ignored the signs and showed up at the office.

This is the kind of position that takes training. Jesus, I can barely lift my head, and now I've gotta learn new nomenclature and algebraic equations, memorize programming, and familiarize myself with pricing structures. It was complete misery. As soon as I could crawl into my bed, I did. This means my eight-year-old put me to bed at night. Fantastic.

We still got her fed and bathed, did homework, and spent quality time together. But she was my caregiver, too. She even offered to take the trash out—for the first time ever. What a little doll. She made me a sundae and was ready for childcare on time every morning with no complaint. She stepped up to the plate.

Being a hard-ass, I never let on to my ex-marine how bad things were. He's feeling pretty guilty about not being around. In his man mind (do not confuse this with a more realistic woman's mind), he was doing me a favor by letting Ella and me get adjusted to our schedule. He should feel guilty.

Our schedule is brutal. She has swimming, Brownies, drama group, and Hebrew school. Add in an hour and a half of homework each night, and you're cooked. How much homework? Half an hour of reading and a full report on the book and pages read. Then we have a page or two of math with graphs, fractions, and multiplication; spelling words; social studies; and—my personal favorite—a study of the moon and its phases.

The moon study is my favorite because when Ella is with her daddy, he calls nightly to ask where the moon is. Dumbass! Did you try looking up? Take your pants off, turn around in front of a mirror, and look behind you. It must be another cock-blocker tactic.

When the child is with me, I often put her to bed before the moon is up. The science teacher is a newbie. She has no kids, and it did not occur to her that the children who get up early for school must go to bed early also. Maybe she's single. Wonder if she would be into CARB? Nah, she may be a little dense, but she's way too cute for him. She's cranky as all get out but vastly more attractive.

Still, we sent Darrin to the Kids' Learning Night. Going without him meant he'd still be grilling me on the finer details. Better to send him. Otherwise, we would have to go together. People would then say, "Look, they are so cute together." Ah, yes. They do this thing. I, however, would do no such thing unless I accidentally signed on for a lobotomy—soul removal and reverse liposuction included. Even then, it would be a stretch.

The school prefers we do not take our kids to curriculum night, so it was easy to stay home with my child. Everyone is happy, and he gets to see what's going on. You've got to put on a show of caring. That's why I help out at the school a lot. Teachers put up with a lot more shit if they get free labor included. It's always best if the talk in the teachers' lounge is positive regarding your family

There were rumors about our family in the teachers' lounge. Luckily, they were only about stupid stuff. Thank goodness they have no real dirt! We'll have to leave that up to someone else. Hanging with kids all day can be tiring. Somebody'd better give these people some good dirt, because they need the excitement.

SEPTEMBER 29, 2008

Monday was a rough day. So, after work, Jax and I met up at O'Toole's. Coupla shots, beers, and what have you later, and this floozy (yours truly) is ripping the guy's T-shirt off him. And that's just what happened at the bar in public. Later in bed, the action was more aggressive. The T-shirt is now in the trash and completely unrecognizable. That's all I've got for good dirt. We got a little dirty.

Lesson 23

THINGS EVEN OUT

OCTOBER 4, 2008

Now, I am sleeping next to my little princess. Things even out. She had a nonsleepover at Jennie's last night. This morning she was all tears and arguments, poor baby. We were going to invite a friend over but thought better of it. God love her, I can barely stand the child when she acts this way. Every statement that comes out of that tiny little mouth sounds like, "Ya wanna make something of it?"

We returned bottles at the grocery store with Jennie and Stacey. It should have been a boring, stress-free errand. Not so much. The girls picked fights. Their hair and teeth were unbrushed. My kid unwisely chose shorts and a T-shirt while the rest of us were in jackets. Half the machines were down because no one empties them at this store. Stacey is in a hurry because she needs to have the van back for her husband to use. Jennie seeks out samples counters and cleans the people out. The whole table full of samples is scarfed down by one greedy little Jennie.

My child is horrified and proceeds to go into a litany of Jennie's wrongs. We are rushing the little monkeys through a throng of Saturday-morning shoppers. We rush, rush, rush, and then Stacey stops and stares at some mundane thing. Then we rush, rush, and rush again. By now, the idiocy is getting to me. The crankiness has rubbed off. It's obvious that we will not be back on time for Brad to get the van back. Why rush now? I already have my bottles returned and have purchased my creamer, lunch meat, and Fruity Pebbles. At least *something* has been accomplished. Add in a little snuggling with the cranky girl, and maybe we are not so darn lazy, after all. Plus, I made it through week two of the temp job. Plus, we got a huge bag of hand-me-down winter clothes.

I would share job stories, but I'm always afraid of getting let go. Flying under the radar is the most prudent course of action. However, I suck at that. Job stories are more humorous when the employee is not terrified of being walked out the door. For example, someone new came in, and my boss went behind a closed door. I smelled trouble. A replacement already. Just two weeks, and ta-ta. Maybe I'm ta-taking things too seriously. Then again, poverty is a serious issue in America.

OCTOBER 5, 2008

Just now beginning to resurface; ignoring those other people and responding only to the chicks. It's week three, and I am still employed. We let go of the other temp. As far as I can see, there may be a couple of main reasons she was offloaded. She was as cute as hell and would not screw the boss. She had a Romanian accent, and the old boys' network was displeased. Or we had an audit scheduled the following Monday, and someone was trying to cover his ass. I'm going with number three. The poor thing was devastated. I didn't even know until the following Monday when there was a new girl at the desk. Well, really it's an old, schlumpy lady. So, that gives more credit to reason number one. No one there is getting blue balls due to temp number seventy. Yep, that makes me temp number sixty-nine.

OCTOBER 12, 2008

So, that would be only three weeks. Later, this will be livable; right now, no amount of drink is going to make it right. Boy, I *must* be depressed, because there is a naked man, a fridge full of beer, a new bottle of whisky, and a brand new dirty movie. Somehow, none of it interests me.

Friday and Saturday were fine. I wasn't home much. Friday was U of M hockey night with Lainie. Then I spent the night at her place, and we hit the U of M game. Or rather, we hit the tailgate party. We never made it into the game. We just had breakfast, lunch, and dinner in the lot under the group's tent.

That evening I went home to get freaky with my man. It wasn't until Sunday morning that I got the message I was unemployed again. On the message, the recruiter stated he didn't know why I wasn't wanted anymore. He just knew there was no need for me to report in on Monday. He was hoping I would call and fill him in on the situation.

If I knew why people were not hiring me, I would not be in this predicament. I would simply change my behavior. The people who choose to hire me all have issues—serious issues. We have drunk womanizers, psychos, and retards. Once again, I get the jobs no one wants and no one stays in. Well, I just added three more weeks of unemployment to the stash—unless, of course, the temp agency has a better idea. Right now, I need to reapply for unemployment. I got word they are adding another extension. Good, because I'm almost done with my first extension.

OCTOBER 13, 2008

Monday evening. One job application, some networking, coupon clipping, picking up around the house, and tearing out invasive plants. It's a start. Grocery shopping and Halloween-costume shopping should round it out. So, when I take my kid to swim class and don't know what group she's in, I shouldn't feel like a slug. There are a whole wad of kids at the pool. I did enough of a workout in the yard to feel justified avoiding the fitness center near to the pool.

Everyone told me I had to get my kid into swim classes. So I enrolled her, and she complains that it feels like school. One must trick this child into learning. When you're doing something fun, it is not reminiscent of boring classes. We will consider this money saved by never enrolling in swim class again.

We have tried ice skating, karate, swimming, cooking, science clubs, roller skating, drama, girl scouts, ballet, tap, tumbling, and Hebrew school. No one can say this mother does not embrace culture and shit. Thank goodness she doesn't have her mom's commitment issues. Hey, wait a minute...

Tomorrow, I will apply at a grocery store that pays more than $7.35 per hour. Why not? Management trainees are paid nineteen something an hour. In addition, I have an application for an administrative assistant to the clerk's office position in a nearby town. Supposedly there's an opening that has not been promised to anyone on the inside.

OCTOBER 15, 2008

Did I mention that I suffer from depression? The kind that makes a person want to curl up in a ball and get swallowed up by the earth? The kind that makes you feel that you cannot go on living this way? Well, that would be me.

Who would *not* feel like the world's biggest loser when they get confirmation every day? Every day I look for work, and every day I am rejected. Every day I build up new hope, and every day my hope is crushed.

What do you do when you have tried everything you know, and you're still kicked? Who would want to get up for another kick in the ovaries? Not me. The breaking point has been hit. I went back to the community college I attended when I was eighteen and checked into getting a nursing degree. The hospitals are the only places hiring. People have to eat, get sick, and die. So, grocery stores and hospitals are doing well. Beyond that, the rest of us are in the toilet. I feel like a pile of shit, spinning and drowning before hitting the sewers.

Lesson 24

EVERYONE HAS A STORY; DO NOT JUDGE BASED ON WHERE YOU WALKED IN

OCTOBER 18, 2008

Hailey's neighbors in Florida have fled the United States. Last night, after several cocktails and hors d'oeuvres, Hailey came back to her own condo and decided to check out the neighbor's place. The neighbors had moved out, but there were still a dozen trees and plants out on their terrace, which connects to hers. So, she crawled over the terrace wall to explore. Well, the unit was unlocked and empty inside. On the dining-room floor was this ripped-open FedEx envelope, and papers were strewn all over. They were demand letters outlining all their debt. Get this—Duane's is in debt to the tune of over $5 million. He owes $75,000 in back taxes from '06 and '07 alone. Interestingly, his "wife" Yvette isn't named on anything. All their cash and probably their new place in the Bahamas are in her name.

Last March Hailey remembers chatting with Yvette, as she packed up their tiny sixty-foot yacht out front at the dock. She said they had decided to move it down to their condo in the Bahamas.

Now it all makes sense. They didn't want the yacht repossessed, and they knew their businesses and houses here were going away soon, so they took off with their dinghy and fled the country. They are no doubt continuing the high life in the Bahamas.

She'll miss Yvette and her broken English constantly complaining about her husband. She was a stunning, tall blonde with the perfect body who appeared to shop till she dropped, drove a little red Porsche convertible (also nowhere to be seen), and hung out at the pool on the phone to her family in Europe the entire time she was at the pool.

Her husband, Duane, was about twenty years older and a hundred pounds overweight, smoked cigars out on the terrace, and was a total dweeb in the personality department. Their stories never matched up. The first-time story they gave was that he was divorced with a couple of kids in college. Next trip down, Yvette was there, claiming she was his wife and there were three kids.

Hailey's story is impressive. Doesn't dude know he's gonna end up in a freezer somewhere before they ever get to the Bahamas?

The fact that my ex quit paying rent almost a year ago seems okay by comparison. And I wouldn't care if I weren't paying the mortgage on the house to the tune of about $20,000 a year, and I stand to rake in a whopping $10,000 at best if employment prospects don't pick up.

This morning, I was talking to my friend Eve about people we know who just quit paying bills. Two of her neighbors stopped paying the mortgage. One left for Canada. One stayed here and didn't file bankruptcy. He stayed in the house for over a year making no payments, but now they're finally garnishing his wages. I'm thinking bad credit is bad credit—may as well take it to the limit. He'll just go underground anyway and do his work without paying any taxes. My cousin Krystal defaulted and bought a better house. Eve's in-laws stopped paying for almost two years, filed bankruptcy, and are now leasing a place right next to their old one.

My plan is to hand my place over to CARB if he'll buy me out at the going rate. We'll see how that goes. Or I'll stay here and pay him what I can afford. That would be less than half of what I pay now and what I'd have to pay to rent a two-bedroom place. Or—I work with MSHDA, the home-ownership counseling program in Michigan, transfer everything to my name, and exercise the option of not paying if that's what I need to do. I may be careening off a cliff, but I prefer to feel as if I'm still in the driver's seat!

OCTOBER 20, 2008

The community-college route is not going to be my best bet. But the counselor had valuable advice when I asked direct questions. I now have more people to call and more avenues to follow. Again, people constantly say, "You're doing everything right." Lovely confirmation, but confirmation does not pay my bills or help me sleep any better at night.

OCTOBER 21, 2008

More job search, more wash, more calls—boring. Today I took a shot with nurse recruiters, the only recruiters you can get through to right away. Other temp-agency recruiters got calls, too. Plus, I applied at the county again and a bunch of other websites. Beaumont hasn't gotten my new info recently. In May, they changed systems, so I'll reapply. A call was also put into Oakland Service Agency and the United Way. My mortgage stuff was sent in today to see if an outside agency would speak to the lender on my behalf. A part of me just wants to let my place fall to hell and say, "Evict me."

OCTOBER 23, 2008

The latest news on reeducation is that the better schools have a two-year waiting period. Sit around and wait for two years? God damn it. This is why I have a better relationship with Jack Daniel's than Jesus Christ.

The good news is that someone is hiring: hospitals. The bad news is that you can't get into the programs required to get jobs at those hospitals. The good news is that some people can get scholarships, grants, and loans. The bad news is that most can't get them before they start a nursing program, and most people can't start the program right away. This all boils down to one thing: I am a serial loser, and I don't know how the fuck my kid and I are going to live.

The other bad news is that soul searching is no fun. The good news is that I still have a soul to search for. It is completely intact. Continuing with the souls-and-spirits theme, I tried to downgrade the liquor. Bad call. Canadian Club and Evan Williams suck. Poor people are not all lazy. But we are tired.

We are tired because our worries about how to pay the bills keep us up at night. Most of us have to get our kids to school and don't have the luxury of sleeping in.

Back to the loser theme, since I am already in a bad place. This suburban house bitch, or bitch in suburbia as I refer to myself (BS for short), is ready to reflect on her past.

Violence against women was acceptable in the home I was raised in. How and why would you raise a little girl to believe that? You push her, you hit her, you chase her, and you demean her. Or you simply stand by and watch while someone else does these things. When violence is a part of your world, you come to accept it. I have a brother and a sister. They learned the same anger-management skills—which is to say, none of us have anger-management skills.

A short stay at the ARK, a center for troubled and displaced children, when I was a young teen occurred because of escalating tensions in my home. I clearly remember the day my brother won his first tussle with my dad. Relief was the main emotion. Joe held him down and asked, "How does it feel, old man?" He also made him say uncle. That was what it took to make my father stop. He needed to understand the powerlessness you feel when someone who is supposed to love and respect you chooses to hurt you instead. And it didn't hurt that my brother told him in no uncertain terms, "You won't do this again."

My brother protected me from danger. That is, until he *became* the danger. My brother took over as the most aggressive person in the household. One night, he got angry that I'd turned on a hall light and began kicking me in the stomach to emphasize his displeasure. Chances are he was coming down from coke and couldn't sleep. Any noise or light sent him into a rage. Jackson and his landscape buddies were guys you did not want to cross.

As a teen, you don't always review the possible consequences to your actions. I crossed him. Or rather, he crossed in front of me. The next day when I was leaving for work in my car, he stood in my path. I revved the engine for emphasis and told him to get out of my way. He didn't move, but my car did. After I hit my brother with a minivan, we stopped. He grabbed the keys out of my hand. We were silent. We were in shock. We were kids, but we knew a line had been crossed.

My boss came to get me and made a safe place for me in her home. I followed through on my commitment to her and her family and stayed on as the nanny until school started in the fall. My boyfriend, who was six years my senior, promised to take me away from all this. He suggested I live with his sister until we could get a place together. We deserved a better life, and we were going to experience it together. His sister would get extra money for rent. He was finishing his MBA, I'd get an associate's degree, and we would live happily ever after.

Happily ever after didn't last long. Once I was escorted away from my family and friends, he became more controlling. In time, he too became violent. As a victim, your head and your body know this to be wrong, but life experience has taught you that this is the way things are. It's all you've ever known.

Of course, I tried leaving. But where was I going to go? Back home? The police are not well equipped to deal with these situations, and they know that victims often return to abusers. They were empathetic, and they did suggest a shelter. And I did go to a local shelter—yet another place for people who have no other place to go. In the end, I moved back home with my abuser.

From my experience, the punching, kicking, and pushing aren't the worst part. The worst thing is the psychological damage. Knowing that the person you have grown to love can hurt you at any time for any reason is horrifying. Knowing there's truly nothing you can do to prevent it is crushing. All the victim can do is wait for the next time it happens. Sometimes we even believe the abuser when they tell us it will never happen again. The good thing about a big blowup is the honeymoon period. No, not the gifts. It's the knowledge that you will have time off because of their last episode of bad behavior.

In the abuser's eyes, it's still the victim's fault, because the victim should know better than to do what makes the abuser angry. The victim should know that the abuser cannot control his or her anger.

My partner hurt me when he *wasn't* angry, too. He threw out personal cards and letters. He didn't pass on messages. He took money out of my purse. He hid things. He just terrorized me. He had favorite games: pouring cold water on me when I showered; waiting until I was in a deep sleep and pushing me out of bed; throwing out my plate as I was eating because, "You're getting fat."

Then he was promoted by his company, and we transferred to another state. All the man needed was a little more rope. Give them more rope, and they will hang you. In my case, he didn't hang me. He choked me. He held me against the wall and told me I could never leave him.

OCTOBER 29, 2008

That's when it clicked. Better late than never. Ginnie and her boyfriend, Kolt, had room for me. Their other flatmate was moving, and they needed the extra money. It was close to work and school, and they were supportive of my choice to get rid of the abusive bastard.

I have a lot of good memories from that summer. Not all of them were good, though. My most vivid memory of that period was of Kolt cleaning his gun as I packed up my things to leave Massachusetts. He was doing this in my presence just in case I tried to steal their stuff or start any funny business. Again, five foot three and a buck four. Did he think I had a switchblade in my shorts? My rent was paid, and everything was in order—they just disapproved of my dating choices. Join the club! I disapprove of my *own* dating choices. They suck!

NOVEMBER 6, 2008

Tonight, Jackson is meeting with a gentleman named Billy whom he used to coparent. All this time, Billy's mother has been telling him that Jack was his father. *Nice.* Tonight, Jax will go out to dinner with Billy and his wife to tell him the truth. He is nervous. He's bringing a copy of the medical tests that prove he is not the baby daddy plus pictures of this kid from birth to almost eight years of age. He's also bringing the picture of himself and Billy's mom at the prom. There is also a picture of the car (a Gremlin) that he and the mom were in the night they were hit by a drunk driver, causing her to almost lose him when she was five months pregnant. That was the night they decided to tell their respective families she was knocked up.

I can almost swallow this information until he pulls out another picture and says it's Billy's aunt. At this point, I say, "Jesus, Jax! You slept with her, too? Get fixed—*now*!" To Jack's credit, he told me these things in the beginning, never expecting them to come up again. So, of course Billy, the long-lost not-son, tracks Jack down and calls him while we're carving Halloween pumpkins with my eight-year-old. To this I say, "Wow, that hooking-up-with-the-single-mom thing is a pretty good shtick!" And then I told him what responsible men are supposed to do with their stick.

NOVEMBER 8, 2008

Friday, I stayed home alone to fill out applications for scholarships. The applications must be in by the fourteenth. I'll drop them off on Monday. Going out would have been a less responsible choice than staying in.

The fake-daddy date went well. Toby and his wife were thrilled that Jackson named the date and place and actually showed up. Next time, they'd like his girlfriend to be there. I'm game. They laughed, they cried, they drank beer—my kind of event.

The date was comfortable, and the mother was not bashed. They each reported on family members. Jackson in turn reported that he plans to marry his girlfriend because he can't imagine spending the rest of his life without her. Maybe it was insensitive to tell him my next book was entitled *Cougar Goes to College*.

NOVEMBER 12, 2008

Recently I've been running around trying to come up with some kind of brilliant survival plan. Nope, got nothing so far—but here's some of the legwork. I had a sit-down with Jax during which I described all my options as I see them. This was done on a large sheet of paper that included pictures of myself living in subsidized housing labeled "Fat Welfare Bitch and Dirty Chilluns." He is also in the picture, literally and figuratively, but I let him draw himself. He drew himself in with large ears, a hockey jersey, skates, and a bulge in his pants. Yup, I made up a map of our future, and he was forced to draw in where he sees himself in my future. "Baby, you scare people" echoes in my head.

Area colleges are holding meetings, and I'm attending them for their back-to-school plans. NWLB (the state of Michigan No Worker Left Behind program) is leaving me behind. It will not pay for prerequisite courses, and every nursing program has prerequisite courses. So, it only pays once you are accepted, and that takes at least a year.

An appraisal was done on the house. It should come back late this afternoon. Darrin offered to pay for it, but he was angry that I didn't have the appraiser call and talk to him first so he could give "vital information." In Darrin-speak, that means pay them extra to get the low number he wants. He tried to sneak this by me, saying he wanted to pay with a credit card because he didn't have money. Really? How big an idiot does he think I am? I told him I'm flush this week with my unemployment check being so large.

I checked into legal aid, and like every other "aid" service out there, I do not qualify until I, or my dependent, lose an appendage due to homelessness and frostbite. You know who *should* be homeless? Bo should be homeless. I spoke with my old employer Bo at BBHS. He wants to make things right and called to tell me so. I told him paying what he owes would get him started on the right road. He has yet another child. The judgment against him can't help his piss-poor credit, and I explained that you can't make a personal judgment go away when you file for bankruptcy. Of course he filed, and he also lost his huge house in White Lake. It could have been beautiful. The landscaping itself was to die for.

I filled out eleven separate forms for scholarships that I can qualify for. That's the good news about my life being so crazy—I have history. For example, to qualify for one of the scholarships, you had to have dated a loser. Check. Extra points if you married him. Check, check. If I could only just get the money and not go to school...nah, that never works out.

NOVEMBER 19, 2008

Last night, I found an attorney who would commit to a pro-bono strategic meeting. The gentleman was intelligent, creative, and informed. My problems are not solved, but I do have a more realistic picture of where I stand legally when it comes to being able to keep my home.

Area schools have been researched and visited. Classes are signed up for. Paperwork for the Federal Work Study program has been filled out. Many scholarship applications have been turned in, and more are on the way. Some schools encourage early applications before prerequisites are filled, so today I'll apply to two of them and write up a plan of action. The transcripts will be sent out and the essays written. In addition, I will apply for a large school loan. We will have to live off that loan. Thank goodness my credit isn't shot yet. Jackson seemed surprised my credit was so good. I was offended until he pointed out that I haven't worked six months straight since the day we met. Good point.

Still, I stay busier than many people with full time jobs. Let's go over this. In the past two years, I divorced my soulless husband and began a job at Weight Loss Giant that paid pitifully. There is a class-action lawsuit in the works regarding their illegal payment system. In short, the company was to pay only for time *scheduled* to work and not the actual time worked. Many employees worked overtime but were not paid overtime. The attorney handling the case has my written statement.

Before the divorce was finalized, I was introduced to scary Scammy—con artist extraordinaire and bad news all around. He found me at a weak point in my life and swooped in, waiting for me to fall down like a wounded creature. He's someone who should be taken out back and shot.

Speaking of being shot, I just got a call from another staffing firm. They asked me to substitute-teach for the Inkster School District. That one needed to be declined due to safety issues. No amount of pay is worth being shot at by your students, their parents, or area drug dealers.

Teaching would be rewarding. What if I started as an adjunct professor in business and moved up to nursing instructor? The adjunct thing is something I could do this summer, but the nursing thing is three to five years out. My guess is that it's best to learn to do before you teach.

Scammy was here for the bad times. I would like to give him credit for that, except, unfortunately, he only made the bad times worse. The words spoken went from "I love you" to "I love Ella" to "I want to marry you." Then he added, "Got any cash for smokes?" and "I promise I will pay you and all your neighbors back." Whoa! It isn't enough to admit that you've scammed me; you have to shame me by scamming my neighbors, too? What a slap in the face. We were all conned. Thank God he left the state.

It takes years to recover from divorce. Emotionally and financially, divorce is draining. Then my dumb ass gets involved with some scammer who drags me down with him all over again. He was never important enough to me to be considered my boyfriend or anyone with long-term potential. But he managed to wreak long-term damage nonetheless.

One example of damage would be the deal Scammy made with my next-door neighbor to buy his Jeep. He drove drunk, damaged it, was arrested, and never paid what he owed. My neighbor had to repossess his Jeep from the dude who was trying to get me to let him move into my house. The car Scammy had before that, he had to give back to his old boss for non-payment. Now, he told me that they had an arrangement. In retrospect, the arrangement probably involved some kind of payment that never happened.

This morning I was making coffee and a bagel, waiting for Darrin and Ella to drop by. He said he didn't have her glasses. He was correct. She'd left them on the baker's rack in my kitchen last night. I put them on the table for her to pick up on the way to school. Some things never change.

Still, some things are ideal just the way they are. Today is my second-year anniversary with Jax. We met two years and four months ago. It took us a little while to decide whether or not to be exclusive. I was against it and held out as long as he would let me.

Today, I called to let him know that I took a part-time (twenty hours per week) contract assignment (two months) in my field. That will give me a little cash. He called back to tell me his plant is closing from December 12 to January 12. GM owes billions of dollars (over $30 billion) to his employer. If GM doesn't pay, his company closes the doors for good. I said I will do anything I can, to which he replied (as usual), "Blow job." Again, it's pleasant to know that some things never change.

I have made some shitty choices. In an ideal world, that would change. C'mon, who wouldn't be frightened? The day Jax and I had our first big sit-down was the Sunday before Thanksgiving. We met up after church, and my friends took Ella for a couple of hours so that we could talk. Yes, we talked. Earlier, he had asked me if I was ready. Correction: he *expected* that I was ready earlier and was wounded when that wasn't the case. Funny how men think women are all dying to be exclusive. Well, maybe I am the anomaly. Maybe other women do want that.

Our first Big Talk was held in the parking lot outside a coffee shop while his daughter babysat mine. Dinner was enjoyable, but I sensed he had something he needed to share. Both of us were surprised. I didn't see it coming, and he didn't anticipate my reaction. To be clear, I didn't know he wanted to be exclusive. So, why not play the field a little longer? It's a numbers game, isn't it?

But the talk got me started weeding out potential boyfriend applicants. Then I began calling some of the men I had been seeing and let them know I was no longer available. Then Jackson and I discussed how we were going to do this thing.

And now, we've been doing this thing for years. To celebrate our anniversary, we had four o'clock cock and six o'clock cock. At his first work break, he called to say we were due for another. So, the sex is still amazing. Emotionally he is right there. Jackson is funny. That's my favorite thing. And he's often helpful. He does dishes, homework, and the floors. He listens, participates, compliments, includes, and respects.

The squirrels are outside collecting leaves for their nests. There is a light dusting of snow on the ground. The leaves crackle in her mouth as the mother squirrel pulls herself up the big oak to line her winter home. She's plump. She's preparing. She expects a hard winter but knows spring will come again. When it does, there will be another new beginning.

Epilogue

My name is Jewel, and I am still holding the pen. The key component of bitch-craft is truth. The hardest part about telling the truth is admitting it. I have issues; my issues include drinking, swearing, and making bad choices. I fuck up on a regular basis. Nevertheless, I do manage to get a few things right. I may not always make the right choices, but I land on the right side of the law and the right side of the grass. Stumble, wildly and wonderfully, into your mistakes, just please, try to avoid mine. Let's go over the lessons learned.

LESSON ONE
JOURNAL

Aunt Pearl and McKenna were dead on; putting your secrets and troubles down in a diary, or with a trusted friend, is safer than acting out. The act of writing things down is also useful in future court proceedings. I would never caution you against marrying a lawyer, but I will say that the financial impact of divorcing one was less than stellar.

LESSON TWO
LEARN FROM THE BEST

If your goal is to be the big dog in the yard, learn from the meanest bitch around. Catherine, Darrin's stepmother, is the epitome of bitch, and if Catherine is not satisfied, there is hell to pay. My own mother is quite different. She has perfected the art of shoving her needs and feelings into a box and, after a lifetime of this, she did not simply misplace the box, she forgot she ever had one.

LESSON THREE
LIFE DOES HAVE A RESET BUTTON

It is never too late to start over. The hardest part of ending a relationship can be admitting failure. Darrin and I are destined for different paths and nothing will change that. When relationships no longer fit; spring clean your social life, with vigor, and without guilt. You have a right to be happy.

LESSON FOUR
ACKNOWLEDGE BOTH HIGHS AND LOWS

Humans only appreciate the sun after the rain. We are stupid that way. Ride the roller coaster of life with your hands up in the air. Do the math; you have survived 100% of your worst days.

LESSON FIVE
LEARN TO RECOGNIZE FUCKTARDS

Narcissists are crafty, toxic people roam the earth, mental illness is real, and not all so-called healthy people are stable. People lie and friends let you down. Privileged people have a tendency to be painfully ignorant and self-aggrandizing at the same time. So, learn to recognize fucktards and keep in mind that you may see them in reflective surfaces.

LESSON SIX
ACCEPT IMPERFECTIONS

Watching someone make efforts to improve is encouraging, and a proper apology includes intent to end the offending pattern. Recognize the difference between a mistake and a pattern. For example, Ella's table manners improved significantly, because she made a concerted effort. She eventually passed that stage and moved on to that teenage, ignorant of the world, insubstantially arrogant one. Mature, loving adults sacrifice for children, and in return, the children condemn their parents in an effort to become independent. It is fucking hateful, but normal. My formal nickname for Ella is Princess Angsty McSullenstein Catalyst of Righteousness, and I plan to love her through it.

LESSON SEVEN
FUCK IT—CELEBRATE IMPERFECTIONS!

No one will ever love you for you, until they know the real you. When I am at my worst, amazing people come out of the woodwork, in support. Life is not about the front you put on; it is about who has your back. Celebrate humanity, especially your own.

LESSON EIGHT
REMEMBER YOUR ROOTS

Catherine shamed Jewel, for being from a small town, in the country. Your past does not define you, yet, the past is part of the person you are. I am proud of my hometown, childhood friends, and the adults who helped shape my formative years. My journey is something to be proud of, from beginning to end. Your journey can be, too.

LESSON NINE
COME BACK WITH YOUR SHIELD—OR *ON* IT

Roman soldiers were told to come back with their shield or on it, before going off to war. Do not be afraid to get bloody, sweaty, and dirty. Bare your teeth and run screaming into the melee. Scars are sexy, because they show that you were tougher than whatever tried to hurt you.

LESSON TEN
THE HEART IS A MUSCLE; IT GROWS BACK

Heartbreak is not a death sentence. As a veritable expert on break ups, I can assure you that you will recover. Heartache changes us, but it does not mean that our hearts must become brittle. Bones break, hearts expand, and like any other muscle in our body, we must break it down to build it up.

LESSON ELEVEN
CLEAN YOUR OWN CLOSET, AND TAKE THE HIGH ROAD

In my metaphorical closet, you will see a rack of self-acceptance issues, right by the shoes. Two glaring words in this text are fake Jew. Jewel desperately tried to be something she was not, thus, she was fake. I was haughty, and I will be damned if I do not know exactly where Ella got that sanctimonious attitude. Karma is a bitch, but so am I.

LESSON TWELVE
RULES NEED NOT BE FOLLOWED BUT MUST BE KNOWN

No one said you have to play by the rules; your task is to know them. You can choose to artfully skirt the rules, or blatantly disregard them. That said, women who throw themselves at other ladies' men, make enemies. Most women find this behavior grasping, desperate, and embarrassing. If you do not wish to get shanked, do not be a skank.

LESSON THIRTEEN
NEVER BE AFRAID TO GET A NEW RIDE OR SIDE HUSTLE

My work history is sketchy. On the bright side, I am constantly learning new skills, having adventures, and meeting interesting people. The only constant in life is change. Something inside me craves that change. Change is my silver lining; nope, it has not lined my pockets, but it has fed my soul.

LESSON FOURTEEN
LIFE IS MORE SOUFFLÉ THAN MICROWAVE MEAL, OR KARMA HAS NO HOTLINE

Everything happens at it's own pace, yet, as a rule, I am impatient. Listening to a person mumble slowly is painful for me, and the stereotypical slow, old man in a hat driver, makes me twitchy. The universe will keep putting the same thing in front of us until we learn the lesson. For example, the universe keeps handing me people like Stacey. I have an attraction to their lackadaisical attitude and sometimes envy their ability to let everything slide, but they also drive me bat shit fucking crazy. Clearly, I am still working on some lessons.

LESSON FIFTEEN
CELEBRATE THE WINS

You know all that hoo-doo voodoo shit about how life is about the journey and not the destination; well, fuck if it isn't true! We tell ourselves that we will finally be happy once we meet some goal. Nope, life does not work like that, so, enjoy the spaces in between. Mini goals are worth celebrating. Every day we are on the right side of the grass is worth celebrating. Do not wait until you have lost those last few pounds, or until work slows down. Celebrate your body, your people, and your life, right now.

LESSON SIXTEEN
DOGGEDLY TRY TO STAY SANE (OR FAKE IT)

In general, people do not know how annoying I find their behavior toward pets. Here is the deal; I love animals, and sometimes prefer them to people. However, I comprehend the fact that pets are not people. So, when humans go gaga over Fido, Fluffy, or Snicklefritz, just let them. They are expressing love.

LESSON SEVENTEEN
GIVE CREDIT WHERE CREDIT IS DUE

Jackson has the patience of a saint. Oh, he falls quite short of sainthood, but he sits back, waits, and watches, without judgement. This man put the friend in boyfriend and the sex in sexy. Jax helped raise Ella while Darrin had other priorities. He taught Ella to tell time, count money, ride a bike, and laugh at herself. Jackson helped hold us together, and he deserves credit for that.

LESSON EIGHTEEN
CALL PEOPLE OUT ON THEIR SHIT
When I am being a douchebag, members of my tribe stage an intervention. True friendship includes the ability to ask your friend if they have considered another, perhaps less damaging option, than your current plan of action. For example, Mac knows me quite well; when I say that I am going to kick something up a notch, she kicks into high gear to stop me. She has learned, from experience, that I have no notches. I go from zero to sixty in seconds flat. There is no yellow caution light, in Jewel's world, so Mac jumps in to urge me to proceed with caution.

LESSON NINETEEN
SMILE AND PRETEND THINGS ARE SWELL
The simple kindness of a smile can breathe life back into a tortured soul. On those few days that I am not smiling, the hallways close in. We are intensely powerful, and sometimes the only muscles we need to flex are muscles in our face.

LESSON TWENTY
STORMS TEACH YOU TO SAIL
We are stronger than the storm; yes, there is strength, even in our weakness. I try too hard, do too much, and can be exhausting. Yet, the vessel I captain is sturdy. No, she is not sleek and will likely not win America's Cup, but my vessel will brave the storm. Storms make us strong, as we learn to navigate through life.

LESSON TWENTY-ONE
SCARE PEOPLE
I am intense; this intensity shows up on paper, and what happens in person dwarfs the paper presence. I scare people. My face is expressive, my body

language screams, and my eyes bore holes. My sarcasm is biting and my humor can be crude and overtly sexual. I am a bitch, but I am a strong, secure, funny ass, sarcastic bitch, and I am enough.

LESSON TWENTY-TWO
KEEP MOVING–YOU ARE LAPPING EVERYONE ON THE COUCH

Life is more marathon than sprint. There are too many people counting on your success for you to give up. Remember, most people want to see you succeed, until your success surpasses their own. This means a few individuals would not mind seeing you fail, and giving them a great big fuck all y'all, will be awesome!

LESSON TWENTY-THREE
THINGS EVEN OUT

We are not the masters of the universe, only a tiny part of it. If you question how insignificant you are to the greater whole, search nature; look down at the grass, up at the trees, view the sunset, and gaze at the stars. Lao Tzu said, "Nature does not hurry, yet everything is accomplished."

LESSON TWENTY-FOUR
EVERYONE HAS A STORY; DO NOT JUDGE BASED ON WHERE YOU WALKED IN

We only see the pages placed in front of us, and this produces a myopic lens. Darrin's actions appear to change as time goes on. This view neglects to take into account how confusing Jewel's change must have been for him. His own lifestyle, choices, and actions remained unaffected by time and parenthood. Darrin's morals were sketchy, but no different from the day Jewel met him. Certainly, the family businesses centered on numerous get rich quick schemes, which were, at best, borderline criminal, but, in his eyes, this lifestyle was what

Jewel accepted. Jewel flipped the script with Darrin; he had no inkling that one day his insecure, submissive wife would go rogue. Action, or inaction, without the motivation behind it, it is only half the story; do not judge based on where you walked in.

About the Author

Like the protagonist in Beginner Bitchcraft, Jewel Albright Cohen has dealt with many trials during her life. She hopes that she is a little more self-aware than her characters are and has a much more mature world view.

Cohen is a part-time professor who has taught everything from advertising to anger management to atoms, and that's just the a's! She is also a feminist, divorcée, serial dater, daughter, sister, and single mother.

Cohen loves nothing more than reading a good book. She hopes that readers can find solace in Jewel's journey and realize how important it is to feel comfortable in their own skin.

www.ingramcontent.com/pod-product-compliance
Lightning Source LLC
Chambersburg PA
CBHW071959170626
46813CB00005B/1926